MW01490122

The Perfect Catch

(The Darcy Brothers)

Alix Nichols

Other books by Alix Nichols:

The Darcy Brothers

The Devil's Own Chloe (prequel)

Find You in Paris (Book 1)

Raphael's Fling (Book 2)

La Bohème

You're the One

Winter's Gift

What If It's Love?

Falling for Emma

Under My Skin

Amanda's Guide to Love

Copyright © 2017 Alix Nichols
SAYN PRESS
All Rights Reserved.

Editing provided by Write Divas

This is a work of fiction.

Names, characters, places and incidents are the product of the author's imagination or are used fictitiously. Any resemblance to actual events, locales, or persons, living or dead, is purely coincidental.

No part of this publication may be reproduced, or transmitted in any form or by any means, electronic or otherwise, without written permission from the author.

Table of Contents

ONE...5

TWO 17

THREE.. 24

FOUR.. 31

FIVE 40

SIX.. 50

SEVEN 60

EIGHT... 70

NINE 77

TEN 87

ELEVEN.. 96

TWELVE 103

THIRTEEN 115

FOURTEEN 125

FIFTEEN 133

SIXTEEN 142

SEVENTEEN...151

EIGHTEEN..156

NINETEEN..165

TWENTY 174

TWENTY-ONE 181

TWENTY-TWO 188

TWENTY-THREE 196

TWENTY-FOUR...................................... 203

TWENTY-FIVE... 210

TWENTY-SIX... 218

EPILOGUE... 222

Author's Note... 228

Bonus Content 230

About the Author.................................. 274

ONE
Noah

I miss Oscar.

The realization occurs to me as I walk across the lobby to the exit of the indoor swimming pool where we train. This morning's practice was focused on sprints, weightlifting, and shooting—in my case, stopping penalty shots. Our coach, Lucas, believes that if I perfect that, it could give the club an edge this season.

I agree with him.

This is why I spent the last hour blocking with every part of my body that happened to be closest to the ball, including my head. A broken nose is a price I'm prepared to pay if it helps my team win.

I step out of the building into the sticky midsummer heat of Paris.

Ugh.

If only I could go back and spend the rest of the day in the pool! Or, better still, I wish the pool would turn into a river flowing from here to the 19th arrondissement.

Wouldn't it be great to just swim home?

Letting out a resigned sigh, I head to my old Yamaha parked on the corner. While I plod there, I picture Oscar bounding up to me and wagging his tail.

After a hard day that starts with practice, then four hours of deliveries, followed by another grueling workout, Oscar is my best sedative.

It'll be hard to unwind when I get home tonight.

And it won't be easier in the morning when I wake up to an eerily quiet apartment. On the other hand, no one will jump on my bed, trail a wet tongue all over my face, and bark until I take him for a walk.

The past two mornings have been the laziest I've had in a year, ever since Oscar turned my bachelor's life upside down. I might have even enjoyed them if it weren't for that stupid plumbing issue in the kitchen.

My sink drain is clogged beyond DIY fixing.

I halt in front of the cafe a few blocks down the street. Ten minutes in an air-conditioned room with a Perrier, an espresso, and a *jambon-beurre* sandwich are just the thing before I jump on my scooter and head to the pizzeria for my shift. That a pro water polo player needs a job on the side is something both the French Swimming Federation and the European Aquatics League must be ashamed of. It's also one of the reasons our national team hasn't won any Olympic medals since 1928.

1928!

Perhaps I should've gone to Italy or Montenegro when I returned to Europe. Or Hungary, for that matter, where water polo is *the* national sport.

The barista hands me my coffee, sparkling water and sandwich while I try to convince my body it doesn't need more to recover from being pushed to its limits at this morning's practice.

To say I'm zonked would be an understatement.

Chewing the last bite of the *jambon-beurre*, I pull out my phone and type a brief message to my new landlord. His family name, by the way, sounds hilarious in French. Luckily for him, he's American—probably of German descent with that name—so it doesn't matter.

> *Dear Mr. Bander,*
> *Could you please send a plumber to fix the clogged drain, or confirm that it's OK if I call one myself? I informed the previous owners about the problem three weeks ago, just before they sold the apartment. Madame Florent didn't have time to take care of it, but she promised she'd let you know.*
> *Many thanks,*
> *Noah Masson*

This is my second missive to him on the subject. If he doesn't reply by Friday, I'll go ahead and call a plumber. I know tenants aren't supposed to take initiative like that without the landlord's prior approval. But how can he give it if he doesn't read his emails?

Still, it would be unwise to antagonize the man. He just purchased the apartment with my lease and has the power to kick me out as soon as it expires.

But I do need my kitchen faucet, dammit.

The one in the bathroom is so short I can't fit the kettle under it. No faucet and no Oscar make me cranky, which might affect my performance. We can't have that. Especially not now, when the team is in its best shape ever and getting ready for the French National Championship and the LEN Cup.

To lift my spirits, I remind myself that Oscar is having a great time now, running free in the Derzians' garden. Lucky bastard. While other dogs—and humans—suffer the heat in Paris, Oscar can breathe. He's spending the whole month at my neighbors' summer house in Brittany with his lady friend, the Derzians' genteel poodle Cannelle.

Oscar isn't genteel, though.

It's anyone's guess what canine *mésalliance* produced the wild combination of traits that is my dog.

He doesn't know any tricks, either.

In short, Oscar is a perfectly untrained brown-spotted mongrel—or a love child, if you prefer—who obeys my orders only when they align with his own desires.

Boy, I miss him.

* * *

When I enter my apartment, half-conscious with fatigue after the shift at the pizzeria and the second workout, my plan for the evening is simple. A cold beer, a bit of TV, and beddy-bye.

Only, there's someone in the kitchen.

Seeing as my landlord is currently stateside and no one else has a key to this place, it can only be a burglar. And with all the noise he's making, a crappy one, too.

I rush into the kitchen.

Oh.

My bad burglar is a woman.

She turns around to stare at me, her right arm still reaching up to open the cabinet where I keep my extra cash.

I make a lunge at her, pull her away from her prize, spin her around, and press her face into the wall. She doesn't offer any resistance, clearly taken by surprise. I shackle her wrists above her head and lean into her to keep her in place.

She mutters something and begins to wriggle. "Let go of me!"

"Not a chance."

She squirms and kicks my shins.

"Stand still until I figure out what to do with you," I say.

She jerks her arms, trying to free her hands.

Good luck with that, chérie. You're up against a guy who spends several hours each day training to improve his grip on a wet ball. And whose single hand is as big as both of yours.

Her next move is to push back.

My response is to press her harder against the wall.

Her ass is out of this world... not that one would normally notice that when restraining an intruder.

It's high.

Round.

Firm.

Perched on top of endless slender legs that I'm sort of squeezing between mine,

As she writhes and pants and I hold her down, a few unusual things occur. My lids grow heavy and my head drops closer to her ash-brown hair that springs in fluffy coils all around her head like a full, soft, warm halo.

The delicious scent coming off it enthralls me. A perfume? Nah, perfumes smell different. Can it be her shampoo, or conditioner, or another beauty product women use to style their hair?

She steps on my foot, hard, breaking me from my trance.

"Ouch," I say, my voice perfectly flat to show her I'm not impressed.

"Let go of me, you stupid man!"

She has a slight accent. American maybe?

"Now, why would I do that?" I tighten my grip around her wrists. "So you can leg it with whatever you've already stuffed into your bag?"

She twists her head to look me in the eye. "I'm *not* a burglar. I'm your landlady."

"Of course." I study her lovely profile. "Pleased to meet you, *Madame*. I'm Snow White and the Seven Dwarfs."

Did I mention her eyelashes are to die for?

Or that she has the lushest, most kissable lips in the universe, topped off by the most beautiful skin I've ever seen. It's smooth, luminous, and the color of coffee with a generous dash of milk.

A light bulb goes off in my head.

This woman isn't real.

She's a fantasy come to life. And not just any fantasy. She's *the* fantasy I've had ever since I hit puberty, come to life.

My free hand twitches as I fight the urge to touch her face.

What the hell.

Feeling this way about this woman is wrong. Not just because I don't know her, or because my mind should be free of any desires unrelated to winning gold in the upcoming season, but because Uma will be arriving in France any day now.

I hope.

"Please, *Monsieur* Masson," she says. "I can explain everything if you'd just stop *hurting* me."

I flinch. Hurting her is the last thing I want to do regardless of who she is and what she was doing in my apartment.

Gingerly, I release her delicate wrists and draw back a notch, planting my hands on the wall on either side of her.

Incidentally, I have a hard-on.

But then again, who wouldn't after a solid minute against a booty like that?

She turns around, jostling within the small space between my arms and chest, and glares.

I narrow my eyes. "So. Let's hear it. Who are you and what are you doing in my kitchen?"

"My name is Sophie Bander," she says, her black eyes boring into mine. "As I said, I'm your new landlady."

Bander.

If she's a thief, how does she know my landlord's ridiculous name? Is it possible she's telling the truth?

"The new owner of this apartment is, indeed, named Bander," I say. "But it's a *Mister* Bander."

She nods. "Mr. Ludwig Bander. I'm his daughter, and *I* am the official owner of this apartment."

Riiiiight.

I swallow and take a step back.

She jerks her chin up triumphantly.

First my ears and then my whole face flame with embarrassment.

I just manhandled my new landlady.

"I'm very sorry about this misunderstanding," I say. "Can we start over?"

Her expression softens. "Go ahead."

I nod a thank-you. "Hello. My name is Noah Masson. I live here."

"Hi," she says. "I'm Sophie Bander. I own this apartment."

"Pleased to meet you, ma'am."

"The pleasure is mine."

We stare at each other.

I rack my brain for something to say and blurt, "My passion is water polo."

"You play professionally?" she asks with a polite smile.

"Yes," I say. "Except, pro water polo isn't like pro football or tennis. Most athletes need a second job."

"Why's that?"

"The level of pay is much lower."

"So what's your second job?" She twists her fingers in her hair. "I bet it's as cool as water polo."

"I deliver pizzas."

"Oh." Surprise flashes in her eyes. "Well, I hope to become a professional, too, one day—in real estate."

"I'm sure you will."

She studies her feet for a moment and then looks up. "*Monsieur* Masson, I think I owe you an apology, too."

"Please, call me Noah," I say.

She nods. "Letting myself in like I did wasn't very professional of me... I should've waited until you replied to Dad's email. Or called me."

I frown. "I don't have your number... And what email are you talking about?"

"My father wrote you that I'd stop by this afternoon to discuss the plumbing problem. Didn't you get his reply?"

I shake my head.

She lets out a sigh. "I bet it's in your spam. Could you do me a favor and check?"

I fetch my phone and open the spam folder.

Smack in the middle of the first page is an unread email from Mr. Bander. So, he did reply to my first email. Only, his letter was sorted with the request to send me a million dollars from Nigeria and an offer for a penis enlargement pill with free shipping.

The subject line of Mr. Bander's note is, unimaginatively, "From Mr. Bander."

I show her the email.

Sophie points an elegant finger at it and shakes her head. "No wonder it went to spam. I *have* warned Dad not to put his name in the subject line when he emails people in France. Guess he forgot."

"Did you tell him why?"

She gives me a hard stare. "No."

I nod in sympathy. In her place, I'd have a hard time breaking it to a parent that his name means "to have an erection" in colloquial French.

"How come your French is so good?" I ask.

"My mom is French."

"Ah, that explains it."

Given that Sophie is a mixed-race chick and her dad sounds Germanic, I assume her French mom is black, maybe of West African or Antilles ancestry.

"I've always lived in the States," she says.

And that explains the accent.

"New York?" I ask. For some reason, she strikes me as a New Yorker.

She smiles. "Key West, Florida. Have you been there?"

I shake my head. Maman and Papa often took me to the US when I was a kid. We visited New York and San Francisco several times. But I have no recollection of traveling to Florida.

My gaze flicks to her lips and lingers there.

She clears her throat. "So, about your drain problem. I was looking for the shutoff valve, so I can give the plumber its location. Do you know where it is?"

"You were close," I say, opening the cabinet next to the one she was about to explore when I came in.

"Great, thank you. I talked to a plumber who can come by tomorrow morning at ten. Will that work for you?"

"That's perfect. I can stop in between my practice and work."

"Is the phone number in your lease contract still good?"

"Yep."

She gives me a business card. "Feel free to email or call if you need something else. I'm here to help."

"Thank you, Ms. Bander," I say. "It's just the faucet. Everything else is in perfect order."

She starts for the foyer then turns around. "Please, call me Sophie."

"OK, and sorry again for the mishap," I say, opening the door.

"It was nice meeting you, Noah." Her lips turn up in a yummy smile. "Despite the mishap."

"You, too."

As her heels clack against the stairs, I wonder how she'd have reacted if I'd answered her earlier question truthfully. I do need something else right now—something she can definitely help me with.

I need to kiss Sophie Bander.

TWO
Sophie

His hard ridge against my backside, imprinting my flesh with its shape...

The scent of his sandalwood aftershave enveloping me...

His face a few inches above mine, his heart racing and his breathing ragged...

The feel of his tall, strong body pressed into mine—broad chest, flat stomach, muscled thighs...

I shake my head to drive away those images. Thoughts of that nature aren't just unusual for me—they're unheard of. They're weirding me out.

Besides, they're totally inappropriate in the workplace.

Grabbing the documents Véronique asked me to photocopy, I scoot down the hallway toward the pair of ever-humming machines behind the cluster of artificial fig trees.

This part of my job sucks.

But hey, I'm an intern and that's what interns do, right?

Except, unlike other interns at Millennium III—the biggest real estate group in France—I have the privilege of owning an actual property in an up-and-coming arrondissement of Paris.

How I convinced Dad to buy me a one-bedroom apartment here is a tumultuous saga that deserves at least three volumes.

The first one would be called *The Impossible.* In this installment, Dad says things like "It's out of the question" and "You're a total rookie with no real knowledge of what this business involves."

The title of Volume Two would be, *Dogged Perseverance and Relentless Nagging* and would cover the period between December and February of last year. That's when Dad resorts to more technical arguments such as "French real estate prices have been stagnant since 2008" and "I'm not convinced about investing in Paris, given the risk of another terrorist attack and how it might affect the market."

I had to dig up data showing that select French cities—in particular, Paris—still delivered a good return on investment. As for my knowing next to nothing about the business, I invoked my GPA as proof of how good a learner I can be.

The third and final installment of the saga would be called *The Impossible Comes True.*

In this volume, Sophie Bander finds the apartment and Ludwig Bander begrudgingly purchases it. They agree that she'll personally manage it during the six months of her internship in Paris from July through December. Then she'll return to Key West, asking Millennium III to take over.

Sophie is ecstatic.

Ludwig is happy that she's happy.

End of Saga.

The photocopier begins to spit page after page into the tray.

As I watch it do its thing, I tell myself I'm lucky in more than one way. My boss here is a top-performing agent who believes interns should do more than make copies or serve coffee to clients. Véronique actually involves me in her real work. Last week, she took me along to show an apartment to a prospective buyer. On Monday, I attended a negotiation. Two days ago, she asked me to draft a lease agreement and compile an inventory.

I had applied for this internship during my final semester in Miami, and received the offer the day of graduation. When I told Dad I was going to spend six months in Paris working for a real estate firm, his eyebrows almost crept under his hairline.

"May I remind you, princess, that *I* own a real estate firm right here in your hometown?" he said, vexed.

"I know, Dad."

"Do you?" He arched an eyebrow. "Do you also remember that I'd be thrilled to offer you a junior position in it?"

I looked down at my feet. "Uh-huh."

"So why on earth do you need to spend six months slaving for someone else in Paris?"

As I searched for the right words, comprehension lit his eyes. "It's your mother, isn't it? You just want to spend more time with Catherine."

His expression softened as he said Mom's name so much so that you'd think he wouldn't mind spending more time with Catherine himself.

But I know better than to nurture false hopes.

It's been several years since I stopped fooling myself that my parents would ever reunite.

Anyway, Dad was right. Being closer to Mom was a big part of why I was going to Paris. I don't see nearly enough of her. Summer holidays and an occasional Christmas or Easter break just don't cut it.

When my parents divorced ten years ago, I chose to stay with Dad in Key West. My friends were there. I loved my school. I loved the weather, the town, and the island.

But that choice came at a price—going through my teenage years without my mom by my side. Oh, we did talk on the phone, daily. We texted, emailed, and Skyped. All of that taken together, I've communicated with Mom a lot more than with Dad over the past ten years.

But all those disembodied conversations couldn't replace the comfort of her physical presence.

I missed those magical evenings, when I'd sit on the front porch to read, and she'd come out with her own book and two frosty glasses of virgin cranberry cooler. I'd move over, and we'd just sit quietly next to each other, sipping our drinks, and reading.

Her Parisian apartment doesn't have a porch or even a balcony. But no matter. I wanted as many of those quiet evenings with her as I could get before returning to Key West and putting my life plan in motion.

Said plan is, by the way, the other reason I'm spending six months in Paris.

I want to learn the ropes of Dad's business. But I want to start by learning them as a regular intern in a big agency where no one knows me, and no one will *go easy* on me. Dad's is the biggest agency in the Florida Keys, but most of his staff have known me since I was a toddler, and all of them treat me like a princess. It's sweet but not very helpful.

The second biggest agency belongs to our main competitor and sworn enemy Doug Thompson. For some weird reason, Doug is extra nice to me. Every time we bump into each other on Duval Street or at Cuban Coffee Queen and he greets me with a warm smile and a "How are you today, Sophie?" I barely nod in response. How can I be friendly with a man who's at war with Dad? Not just a rivalry, but a real merciless, no prisoners, no cease-fires, no-holds-barred war for dominion over the Keys.

Needless to say, applying for an internship with Doug wasn't an option.

I stick the scanned contracts into a manila folder and remove the staple from the asbestos survey report for copying.

As I feed it into the machine, I recall my last words to Dad before boarding the plane to Paris. "Six months is nothing in the big scheme of things. I'll be back before you know it."

His eyes drilled into mine. "Will you?"

"You bet." I gave him a bear hug. "I'll become a real pro and I'll make you proud."

He ran his hand over his close-cropped salt-and-pepper hair and wished me a good trip.

My heart pinches.

I love that man more than the world. What a shame his marriage fell apart!

Since Mom left, I spent countless hours poring over her and Dad's Parisian Polaroids from before I was born. The pics show an ethereal northern blonde and a strapping black dandy posing on Champs-Elysées, in Tuileries, in front of the Louvre, and in other landmarks of the French capital. They hold hands. Sometimes his arm is wrapped around her shoulders and hers around his waist. In my favorite picture they gaze into each other's eyes with such passion you'd think nothing could kill it.

I've never felt as much as a spark of passion for anyone, no matter how hard I tried.

Just as well—no good comes of it anyway.

I wonder why thinking of those old photos has reminded me of yesterday's encounter with Noah Masson. The man is eye candy, no doubt. But beyond his height and athletic build, my blue-eyed tenant looks nothing like Dad.

Not to mention that no one in their right mind would call me a northern blonde.

And yet... what is it about Noah that made me spend an hour last night looking for a mistake in his rental agreement that would warrant a revision? I ended up finding it—*qui cherche trouve*, as Mom likes to say. The previous owner had leased the apartment as unfurnished, even though she'd equipped it with everything from a bed to a vacuum cleaner. Dad bought it together with all the movable property, and Noah's new contract is for a furnished lease. But we'd neglected to change the notice period from three months to one.

While the copier reproduces the termite survey, I pull out my phone and tap.

> *Hello,*
> *Can I stop by around 8 p.m. next Monday to discuss a small change in the rental contract and sign a new copy?*
> *Best,*
> *Sophie*

THREE
Noah

Lucas waits until the last man is in the debrief circle before he tut-tuts. "Four exclusion fouls, people. That's four too many."

We fake remorse the best we can. But we know that, in truth, the coach is happy with the game and proud of us. No amount of tut-tutting can disguise the glee in his eyes.

"Jean-Michel, Denis, your sprints need work, but good effort there." He turns to Zach. "Very good effort."

Zach—our center forward responsible for two of the exclusion fouls—wipes the pretend guilt off his face and grins.

"If you guys can stay committed," Lucas says, "you'll peak right in time for the national championship."

"We're totally committed, Coach," Zach says.

"We'll do what it takes," Denis chimes in.

Valentin, Jean-Michel and the rest of the team shout things like "Hell, yeah!" and "You can count on us!"

"That's the spirit." Lucas turns to me. "Great job with the saves, Noah. Perfect. Technically, tactically—you nailed it. Give me more of the same in the championship and LEN Cup games, and I'll be a happy camper."

Lucas no longer bothers to hide how happy he is. And so he should be. The squad is in great shape. For the first time since Lucas started the club, we're truly ready to fight for gold medals, both French and European. That we just won a scrimmage game against one of the country's best clubs, annihilating them like they were a college team, is no stroke of luck.

"OK, back into the water now!" Lucas blows his whistle. "Chop, chop! Thirty minutes of shooting, followed by thirty minutes of strokes and lunges."

Valentin shifts his weight from one foot to the other. "It's my mom's birthday today. I was hoping to leave in time for the family dinner."

"Do you want that gold medal—yes or no?" Lucas gives our defender a hard stare.

"Yes," he mutters.

Lucas jerks his chin at the pool.

Valentin nods resignedly and jumps in.

When the workout is over, the team—minus Valentin—head to the nearest bar for the customary drink. Zach comes along, too. He's never available in the evening, so I look forward to chatting with him.

Call me a fanboy, but the guy *is* one of a kind.

Just a few years my senior, he's so together it's unbelievable. In the field, he's efficient and generous. Even though he's our hole player, count on Zach to go for an assist over a direct shot, if he believes the team would have a better chance of scoring that way. In addition to being our top scorer and team captain, he also runs a successful e-commerce business and raises a special-needs kid.

Alone.

Maybe he's found the secret to bending space-time.

"How much do you sleep at night?" I ask Zach after everyone has settled around our usual table and Lucas has ordered a round of drinks.

"Six hours," Zach says. "Why?"

I shrug. "I just don't see how you can do all of the things you do and find time to sleep."

"I have help."

"Dobby?"

He chuckles. "Nanny. She's the one who looks after Sam from eight thirty to six. So I can play water polo and operate my business."

"I see."

A crease appears between his brows. "Thing is… I know it's selfish, but I do wish she didn't have kids of her own."

"Are you into her?"

"No!" He laughs. "She's married and she's in my employ. So no way. It's just… If Sam had a live-in nanny, my mornings would be a lot less stressful. And I could go out in the evenings, maybe even date someone."

"How long has it been since you—"

"Long," he cuts in before I can finish.

"You should contact an au pair agency," I say.

Zach shakes his head. "Mathilde has been with Sam for the past three years. She's doing a great job, and Sam is attached to her. The only way I'm hiring an au pair is if she quits, which I hope she won't."

Lucas raises his glass. "Here's to *Nageurs de Paris,* the best water polo club in France! Let's prove it to the rest of the country this year!"

Everyone cheers and chugs their drinks.

Zach turns to me. "What's up with you? Last time we talked, you were mad at your oldest brother for bugging you, and hoped your childhood friend would get her French visa."

"I'm still mad and still hoping," I say with a sigh. "Just as it looked like Sebastian might have given up, his wife took over. She writes *letters* to me. What do you make of that?"

Zach grins. "Like, real letters? On paper?"

"Yep. And she encloses photos with them."

"Of what?"

"Family gatherings. Portraits of my brothers and their babies. That sort of stuff."

Zach gives me a funny look, like he wants to say something but doesn't dare. I told him about my fucked-up family months ago. He knows I was born a d'Arcy du Grand-Thouars de Saint-Maurice. He knows why I prefer to go by Maman's maiden name and why I won't talk to my brothers.

So why that look?

"Don't you think…" He hesitates. "Don't you think your family deserves a second chance? Don't you want to meet your nephew and niece?"

"They're cute in Diane's photos—but no, thanks. I want nothing to do with the d'Arcys."

"What about your friend's visa?" Zach asks, clearly sensing that a change of topic is in order.

I roll my eyes. "The French consulate in Nepal is taking its sweet time."

"I can't imagine she's a security threat."

"Just the usual red tape," I say with a dismissive wave. "But my mother is pushing for her protégée, and my mother doesn't give up until she gets what she wants."

"That explains your brothers' doggedness," Zach says. "It runs in the family."

As much as I hate to admit it, he does have a point.

"It's kind of your mom to take an unrelated young woman under her wing," Zach says. "She's covering all the expenses, right?"

I nod. "Strictly speaking, it's the Marguerite Masson Foundation, of which she's the founding CEO."

"Respect."

"She loves Uma," I say. "You see, Maman always wanted to have a girl, but she had three boys instead."

"I never wanted to have anything." Zach lifts his eyes to the ceiling. "But, thank you, Lord, for giving me a boy. Girls are the sweetest thing, except I wouldn't know what to do with one."

I smile. "Uma is certainly sweet, but she has a backbone and an independent streak. She plans to find a job as soon as she gets here so she can repay Maman."

"Good for her."

"She's willing to wash dishes in a restaurant, clean houses, anything. I'm keeping my eyes open for announcements."

"I'll do the same." Zach glances at his watch. "Got to go. Mathilde has granted me two extra hours, but my time's up."

He fist-bumps the players, shakes hands with Lucas, and heads out the door.

The rest of us stay for another hour, speculating about which club we'll be playing against in the first round of the national games. We also discuss the strengths and weaknesses of the top clubs and their players.

Barring Lucas, I'm the go-to guy on the attackers' preferred shooting techniques, since I spend several hours a week studying them on tape.

As a goalie, you have to.

But the moment I leave the bar, my neurons settle into a new formation, and all I can think of on the ride home is Sophie's text message. My new landlady has found an error in the lease agreement. She wants to discuss it and sign a new contract. Is this a pretext to raise the rent? Or to get rid of me so she can occupy the apartment herself?

My gut tells me there's more to her initiative than just correcting a spelling mistake in the agreement. And I'm going to find out tomorrow if I'm right.

The weird thing is that I look forward to her visit more than I'm apprehensive about it. Actually, "look forward" is an understatement. I'm thrilled. There's this wild idea that's formed in the most primitive part of my brain. I've been trying to dismiss it as wishful thinking—and failing miserably.

What if the sexiest woman to walk the earth has invented an error in the agreement so she can see me again?

What if I'm not the only one who nearly lost it from our brief physical contact the other day? What if Sophie felt the same way and has been lusting after me ever since?

That's preposterous. I know.

And yet I doubt I'll be able to sleep tonight.

FOUR
Sophie

I ring the doorbell.

My white blouse is all buttoned up and tucked into my gray pencil skirt, and my new hairstyle is a lot more sober than the afro I had before. This morning, I spent two hours at my local Salon de Coiffure to get my curls tamed into a classy braided bob.

Until a minute ago, I also wore thick frame fake glasses. According to Sue, my bestie, they transform me from a twenty-four-year-old intern into a twenty-five-year-old yuppie. But I just took them off and shoved them into my briefcase. *Yes, a briefcase!*

I don't really know why.

"Your hair is different," Noah says after I step in and we exchange polite greetings.

Oh, shoot. He doesn't like it. *Not that I care, of course.*

"It's beautiful," he adds, giving me an appreciative nod. "Is this your usual hairstyle?"

"A special effort for my mom," I say. "She's crazy for small box braids."

It's true—Mom loves the look of "easy chic" this style gives me.

What I failed to mention is the last time I had the patience to get Mom's favorite hairstyle was three years ago. And now, this morning.

"Is that how she wears it, too?" Noah asks.

"My mom?" I snort. "She'd love to, but Caucasian hair gets way too damaged from box braiding."

He gives me a confused look. "I'd assumed your mother was black."

I blink. "Why?"

"Because…" He screws up his face as if to say, *Help me out here.*

I frown and raise my brows. I have no clue what he's struggling with.

"Because…," he tries again.

I nod supportively. "Yeeess?"

He gives a shy little smile that could charm a corpse back to life. "Because your dad is named Ludwig Bander?"

I crack up. "You're not the only one to assume he's white."

"He's not?"

"Nope. But there's an explanation."

"I'm all ears."

"When Dad was born, Grandpa wanted him to have a king's name. So, he looked up all the kings who came into the world on the twenty-fifth of August."

"And he found a Ludwig?"

"Exactly. King Ludwig of Bavaria, born on the twenty-fifth of August eighteen something something."

He cocks his head. "Did your father name you Sophie after a queen born on the same day as you?"

"Very smart." I bow in mock admiration. "Princess Sophie. That's what he calls me, by the way."

"Was it the only royal name available for your birthday?" he asks. "Not that I have anything against Sophie. It's a lovely name."

"The other option was Marie Antoinette, but Mom said, 'Over my dead body'."

He gives me a wink. "She should've said, 'Over my *guillotined* body,' given our last queen's unfortunate ending."

I giggle but force myself to stop, remembering I'm here on business in my capacity as his landlady.

It's time I started acting like one.

"How's your sink?" I ask.

"As good as new. Thank you so much for your help!"

"It's my job."

For a brief moment, we stare into each other's eyes as the air grows thick with something unspoken and totally inappropriate.

"Can I offer you a cold drink?" Noah asks, shifting his gaze to his hands.

"A glass of water would be great."

He strides into the kitchen and fills two glasses with water. Then we sit down at the table and I explain the change in his contract.

Noah's gray-blue gaze is locked on my mouth the whole time.

"So, are you OK with the new terms?" I ask when I finish.

He gives me a funny look. "Are you planning to reclaim the apartment?"

"No."

"Because if you are," he adds, "just tell me so I can start looking for a new place."

"I don't have a hidden agenda, really."

I hope he can see I'm telling the truth.

Noah stares at me as if gauging my sincerity and then nods. "OK."

"OK?"

"Yeah, I believe you." He picks up the pen I'd set on the table. "Where do I sign?"

I point at the last page. "Here, please, on both copies."

Thirty seconds later, I rip up the old agreement and push one of the new copies toward Noah. "For your files."

"Thanks."

I stick my own copy in the briefcase.

We're done. My business here is finished, and I can go home.

I *should* go home.

"More water?" he asks, pointing at my empty glass.

"I'm good, thank you."

Both etiquette and common sense dictate that I leave now. Which is exactly what I'm going to do. Soon.

The moment he stops looking at me like that.

Any second now...

"Did Mr. Bander buy a second apartment for you in Paris or are you renting?" he asks without taking his eyes off me.

"I'm renting."

"In this arrondissement?"

"In the 18th."

"Do you like it?" he asks.

"The part where I live, yes. Very much. Do you know rue des Batignolles?"

"Uh-uh."

"It's lovely. I'm close to my mom's place, not far from work, and within walking distance from Montmartre."

"Sounds like the perfect location," he says. "My first year in Paris, I lived in the 18th, too."

I release a frustrated damn. "So much for my good ear for French accents! I'd pegged you as a Parisian."

"Your ear *is* good," he says. "I spent the first eight years of my life between Paris and Burgundy. Then Maman and I moved to Nepal."

"Nepal as in the country in the Himalayas?"

"Yes," he grins. "That one."

"Wow," I draw out. "Was it hard living there so far from home?"

"I didn't mind once I stopped missing my b—"
He stops himself and his expression hardens.
"France."

"Were you in the capital city?"

His face relaxes into a smile again.

That smile will be the death of me.

"Nepal's capital is called Kathmandu," Noah says. "And yes, we stayed there most of the time. Maman and I enjoyed a lot more comfort than the vast majority of people she was helping."

"Did she volunteer for a nonprofit?"

"She still does."

"You must be very proud of her."

"I am."

There's another stretch of silence, during which we stare at each other without uttering a word. Forgetting about decorum, I let my gaze caress his strong neck, firm jawline, and chiseled mouth before it reaches his eyes the color of the ocean on a rainy day.

Our gazes meet.

My heart races—faster, louder—until it starts to feel like a countdown timer in my chest.

What's happening to me?

Come on, Sophie, you're smart enough and big enough to know.

It's called sexual attraction.

Something I've never experienced before. Something I thought was beyond my reach. Which was fine by me, because—let's face it—what good has lust ever done anyone?

Lechery has ruined brilliant careers. Randiness has pushed people to make irrational decisions. Passion has messed up so many perfectly happy, accomplished lives... and for what? A moment's gratification?

My inability to be sexually aroused isn't a flaw as I've come to realize.

It's a blessing.

"Got to go," I say, standing up. "I need to hit the shops before they close."

Noah stands up, too. "Looking for something specific?"

"Folding chairs. I'd like to buy two inexpensive folding chairs for my studio apartment and a bright-colored poster to give it some personality."

"Do you know where to look for that sort of stuff?"

I nod. "BHV."

"BHV is pricey."

"So is everything in Paris."

"But not outside of it." He gives me a mysterious smile. "Have you been to Les Puces of Saint Ouen?"

"What's that?"

"A huge flea market north of Paris, next to the Porte de Clignancourt. If you want items with personality, that's where you should look."

"I would need a car to go there and I can't drive in Paris. Neither can Mom."

"Two folding chairs and a poster, eh? Is that all you need?"

I nod.

"Does your poster have to be big?"

"No."

"Then I have a solution."

I raise my eyebrows.

"My scooter," he says.

"It's kind of you, but if I won't dare to drive in Paris, I'm definitely too chicken to ride a—"

"That's not what I meant. I'll take you to Les Puces."

My jaw slackens. "You can't be serious."

"Why not?"

"Aren't you busy enough with your own life and obligations?"

"It's no trouble at all." He smiles brightly. "I've been meaning to go there, anyway. A friend told me about this bistro, Chez Louisette, where you can eat overcooked lentils, drink cheap beer, and listen to terrible covers of Edith Piaf songs."

My lip curls. "You make it sound so *enticing*."

"Trust me, it's great fun. Besides, now is the perfect time for me to visit Les Puces of Saint Ouen."

"Why's that?"

"I'm grounded in Paris between two water polo seasons, and I can't think of a better plan for next Sunday."

I hesitate.

"Listen," he says. "Will it help if I tell you I have a vested interest in taking you to Saint Ouen?"

"Maybe… Go on."

"I see it as a unique opportunity to ingratiate myself with my new landlady. Who knows, I may never get another chance."

I raise both my hands in defeat. "OK, you convinced me. What time?"

"Nine thirty in the morning. I'll pick you up if you text me your home address."

"Texting as we speak."

I fish my phone out of my briefcase and a few seconds later, Noah's phone beeps with my message.

This isn't wise, Sophie, the voice of reason whispers in my head.

Don't I know that? I whisper back.

A Sunday outing with my sexy new tenant is as ill-advised as it gets.

But, man, I'm excited about it.

FIVE
Noah

Maman video calls me via Skype over breakfast.

I mute the radio, prop my tablet up, and answer the call.

"*Bonjour, mon chéri,*" Maman says.

Her hair, clothes and makeup are as impeccable as ever.

"*Salut, Maman.*"

"I've missed you."

"I miss you, too, Maman."

"My sweet little boy." She gives me a smile tinted with nostalgia. "All grown-up and handsome. Just look at you."

I clear my throat. "Shouldn't you be at the office, bossing people around right now?"

She sighs. "I should, but… I took a day off."

"Are you OK? Migraine?"

"Yes." She rubs her left temple. "Uma's latest news triggered it."

My heart skips a beat. "Did something happen to her? Is she all right?"

"She's OK." Maman gives me a funny little smile. "But she must get out of here real soon. Sooner than we thought."

I sit back, waiting for details.

"Mr. Darji told her over dinner last night he'd been approached about her and expects her to be married by October."

"What?"

She rubs her forehead. "I knew this would happen. Last time I paid them a visit, Mrs. Darji said something about Uma being ripe for marriage, but I hoped it was just a general observation."

Uma is twenty-three, so by Nepali standards, she's close to *overripe*.

"But what about her plans? I thought the Darjis were proud of her talent, and that she was going to Paris to learn haute couture embroidery."

"They were," Maman says. "And now, all of a sudden, they aren't anymore. I had the most unpleasant conversation with Mr. Darji after Uma called me earlier tonight. She was on the verge of a meltdown, the poor thing."

"What did Mr. Darji say?"

"That the man who approached him about Uma is a Brahmin."

"Shit."

Maman smirks. "Certainly not from Mr. Darji's perspective. To him, it's a chance of a lifetime and an honor. You should've heard him rave about the match. How do you reason with someone who's ecstatic?"

I can't say I'm surprised. Brahmins are the high aristocracy in Hindu societies, and the Darjis are Dalits—one of the lowest and poorest castes. Mr. and Mrs. Darji love their children, but I've always suspected their letting Maman encourage Uma's dreams wasn't because they believed in the economic emancipation of women. They just thought that beautiful, educated Uma was too good for street peddlers and manual workers of their own caste.

And then a Brahmin comes along.

No wonder he's ecstatic.

I exhale a heavy breath. "Does Uma want to marry the man?"

"Absolutely not!" Maman bugs her eyes out for emphasis. "She dreams about Paris, the Ecole Lesage, and…" She gives me that funny look again.

"What?" I prompt.

"She's in love with you," Maman blurts out.

For months now, there have been hints and allusions, but it's the first time Maman has actually said it.

I tilt my head to the side. "Oh, come on. We've been friends for years. I'd know."

"No, you wouldn't. Men are terrible at *knowing* things like that."

"What are you saying, Maman?"

"Nothing. Just that I've suspected for a while now that my lovely protégée is enamored with my darling boy." She hesitates. "I'd be just as ecstatic as Mr. Darji, if it turned out the feeling was mutual."

At a loss for words, I blink and stare at her.

This conversation starts to feel like the dreaded game situation when I'm on the wrong side of the goal cage with the opponent's top scorer at the two-meter line, and not a single defense player around to give me a hand.

Fortunately, I'm not in the pool right now.

I can dodge the ball.

"Can you speed up her visa?" I ask. "Is Uma prepared to go against her father's wishes?"

"To answer your first question, yes, I can. Remember *Monsieur* Strausse from the consulate?"

"Not really."

"Anyway, I'm going to call in a favor." She clenches her jaw. "Uma will have her visa next week."

"What about Mr. Darji's consent?"

She studies her hands. "Uma hopes the two of us can persuade Mrs. Darji, and that the three of us can make Mr. Darji change his mind."

"But you don't believe that, do you?"

She gives me a pleading look. I know that look. It was what I'd get every time I asked for more details about my father and my brothers. Especially Sebastian.

Maman told me once, five or six years ago, that it hurt too much to talk about it. Didn't I have all the facts? Didn't I *know* what my father had done to her, and how my older brothers took his side so he wouldn't disinherit them? Wasn't that *enough?*

She was right, of course. It should be.

I mean, it *is*.

Just as I'm about to say bye, Maman purses her lips, and her gaze hardens. "No, I don't believe we can convince Mr. Darji. I don't even think we can sway his wife. They see this proposal as a gift from the gods."

"So what will Uma do?"

"Why don't you call and ask her?"

"I will."

She nods and a few minutes later we hang up.

I finish my breakfast with a lot less appetite than before Maman's call.

When I get to the pool, it turns out I may not be the only one with bad news today. At least that's what the look on Zach's face suggests, as he jumps into the water fifteen minutes after the practice has started.

Zach's *never* late.

"You OK?" I ask him when Lucas lets us rest a few minutes between leg conditioning and shooting drills.

He nods. "I'm fine. It's… I'll explain later."

Lucas blows his whistle, and Zach mucks up his first try from a perfect position. He mutters a curse before picking up the ball again and slamming it with all he's got. I jump high out of the water and block it. His next shot is going to be a lob. That's bad news for me, because Zach is one of the rare players who is able to do it right.

He throws, netting the ball.

By the end of the practice, he's fully recovered his legendary control, and the coach's face relaxes visibly as a result. Small wonder. Our captain isn't just our club's best scorer. He's quite possibly the best shooter in France and one of the best in Europe. While my moniker is "The Rock" due to blocking talents, we call Zach "The Nuke" as in a weapon of mass destruction.

"Is it Sam?" I ask him in the locker room. "Has he come down with something?"

He shakes his head. "Sam's fine. It's his nanny."

I raise my eyebrows. "Mathilde the Perfect?"

"Mathilde the Perfect is cutting her hours in half starting Monday," Zach says with a sigh. "I'll have to miss the afternoon practice, and possibly sit out the season. I'm at my wit's end."

"Doesn't she owe you a longer notice?" I tie the laces of my sneakers. "Is something wrong with one of her own kids?"

He rakes his hands through his hair. "Her older son has been hanging with the worst cads at school. Almost got expelled last week for something that upsets her so much she won't even talk about it. The kid's only thirteen."

"Shit."

"She's cutting her hours so she can spend more time with her children."

"Can she afford it?"

"Unfortunately for me," Zach says with a smirk, "she can. Her husband is a security guard at a shopping mall, and he's about to get a promotion, so they'll manage."

"Hey, you should see this as an opportunity to get that au pair you've been thinking about!"

"Your friend Uma," Zach says. "Did she get her visa?"

"Not yet, but she will in a few days."

"You said she'd be looking for a part-time job as soon as she gets here, right?"

"Oh, I see where you're going with this," I give him a happy grin. "She will, indeed."

"Mathilde will keep the mornings, so I'm looking for an au pair to babysit Sam in the afternoon."

"Uma will be attending embroidery classes at the Ecole Lesage in the morning, and she'll be free in the afternoon," I say. "It's perfect."

"Do you think she'll do an occasional evening, too, so I can go out and 'get a life,' as you put it?"

"I'm positive. Uma's your man... er... woman," I say. "She's great with kids."

"Does she speak French? I'm afraid Sam won't understand any Nepali and his English is very limited."

"She speaks perfect French, as it happens. She went to the same Lycée Français as me, thanks to Maman's Foundation."

Zach expels a relieved breath. "So, you think she'd be interested."

"I'll ask her later today, but I'm sure she'll be thrilled."

"Tell her she'll have a big sunny bedroom, between Sam's room and the guest bathroom. We'll sign a standard contract, and I'll pay her cash for every extra hour."

I nod. "We'll tell her parents she'll be working for a family, OK? If any Nepalis call your house, you're *married*."

"No problem." Zach smiles. "I totally get how that would reassure her parents. If necessary, I'll ask Colette to play along and talk to them over Skype when she stops by to visit Sam."

"She won't mind?"

Zach has maintained a good relationship with his ex for Sam's sake, but I doubt she's a generous kind of person.

"She'll do it," Zach says.

"Cool."

He gives me a suspicious look. "Is there something going on between you and Uma that I should be aware of?"

The question is so unexpected I lose my tongue.

"I didn't mean to pry," Zach adds quickly. "And you're free to say it's none of my fucking business. It's just… as her future employer and your friend, I'd like to know if she's *more* than a friend to you or *used to be* more than a friend. To avoid gaffes or awkwardness."

"It's a fair question," I say. "We've never been romantically involved. But we used to be close growing up. She's a fantastic human being."

Zach cocks his head. "Is that a roundabout way of saying you'd like to be romantically involved with her?"

I remember Maman's statement that Uma is in love with me. Could she be right? What about me? Do I love Uma more than just as a friend?

"Relax." Zach pats my shoulder. "I'm her future employer not her older brother."

I pick up my duffel bag and stand. "If I were looking for a relationship, I guess Uma would be perfect. My mother certainly thinks so."

"Well done, buddy!" Zach grins. "You haven't even started dating the woman, but you already have your mother's approval." He stands and slings his duffel over his shoulder. "For what it's worth, you have mine, too."

"That's great." I give a tight smile. "But I'm not looking for a relationship at the moment. I want to focus on the games."

Which is why the attraction I feel for Sophie is best ignored.

Offering to take her to the flea market on Sunday was a deplorable lapse of judgment. But it's too late to call it off now. I'll be fine. I'll do my duty as a good tenant, making sure to keep it friendly and professional the whole time. And after we say good-bye, chances are we'll never see each other again.

"Oh, yeah, absolutely," Zach says. "I want to focus on the games, too. But I do look forward to having an au pair in the house so I can date again."

I give him a sympathetic smile.

"That is," Zach adds, "if I can figure out the new dating rules and remember how to ask a woman out."

It's my turn to pat his shoulder. "Fret not, my friend. I happen to know a hot single woman who might be exactly what you need."

The moment those words are out, I wish I could take them back. A jealousy I've never felt for anyone before stirs deep inside me. It makes me feel like a character in the *Alien* movies who discovers that a horrible creature has quietly hatched and grown inside his gut.

The beast thrashes in anger and pain, roaring, "Sophie's mine!"

What the fuck?

"That would be fantastic!" Zach turns to me, his eyes bright. "Do you think you could arrange a chance encounter?"

"Sure thing." I force a smile even as the alien bellows so hard I can barely hear myself speak.

SIX
Sophie

"Hop on," Noah says, handing me a helmet and jutting his chin to the spot behind him.

The only thing his scooter has in common with the sleek two-wheelers Parisians favor is its general shape and presence of a motor.

"Did you find this... *thing* at Les Puces?" I ask, climbing on behind him.

"Don't worry," he says. "It's in a better shape than it looks."

Once I've adjusted the helmet, I put my arms around his waist, and off we ride into the hubbub and exhaust fumes.

By the time we're on the Périph'—the main ring road around Paris—I'm a wreck.

I knew the journey would be rough because of all the noise, traffic, and pollution along the way. Specifically, I'd anticipated muscle pain in my neck and shoulders because I'd spend the entire ride tense with fear that we would collide with a truck or fly off our iron horse on a sharp turn.

But an altogether different fear stiffens me.

As we slalom between cars, buses and bikes, I worry Noah could hear my heart pounding like crazy in my chest. What if he misinterprets it? What if he assumes I'm squeezing his hips between my thighs *not* because I'm hanging on for dear life, but because I enjoy the contact? The embarrassment of it! Just to think he might imagine that the constant friction between said hips and thighs excited me.

It does not.

And what if he assumed the reason I'm hugging him tight, my breasts flat against his back and my cheek pressed to the back of his neck, is not to increase my chances of survival, but because he aroused me?

He does not.

Nobody does.

What I'm feeling is adrenaline—not arousal. There's no way it's arousal. I don't *do* arousal. Never felt it before and not going to start now. Besides, the way I envision my future, I have no use for it.

Twenty or so minutes later, Noah turns off the Périph' and parks the scooter in front of a row of bric-a-brac stalls.

"*Et voilà,*" he announces removing his helmet. "Welcome to Les Puces of Saint Ouen!"

I hand him my helmet and look around. "Where's the entrance?"

"Here," he says pointing to the cluster of scruffy peddlers selling knock off watches and handbags.

"Is this some kind of Platform Nine and Three-Quarters, and we're supposed to walk right through these people?"

He chuckles, shoving our helmets into the saddlebag. "I suggest we go around them. There'll be two or three pretty gates inside the market."

"Promise?"

"Cross my heart."

"All right, then."

"Shall we?" He motions toward the stalls. "We have a lot of ground to cover."

I nod and follow.

For the next hour, we wander between booths displaying old stamps, kitchen gizmos, costume jewelry, vinyls, and all sorts of knickknacks. To some of these items, time has been as kind as to Jane Fonda. Others haven't aged quite so well.

I halt in front of a small boutique that sells vintage wedding dresses.

Ooh-la-la, they're pretty.

I'm not speaking about the 80s monstrosities with puffy sleeves and nylon skirts whose white has veered to gray. What I'm gawking at are the cream-colored ones cut in raw silk and lace.

The day I marry the man of Dad's dreams, I'll wear a dress like this.

When we pass a stand with dozens of severed doll heads organized by size and color, I wince and glance at Noah.

He shrugs. "To each his own bad taste."

"Let's move on," I say. "They creep me out."

"Did you know this is the largest flea market in the world, and one of the oldest?" Noah asks as we amble on.

"Really?"

"It was established back to the 1880s by ragmen called *biffins*."

I quirk my lips. "Someone's spent time reading up."

"Just doing my job as your guide for the day."

Another hour of exploring the main artery of *Les Puces* called rue des Rosiers, and the alleys that branch off it, and I find what I came here for. Actually, Noah was the one to spot the booth selling framed vintage posters. I picked an adorable, red and white *affiche* of a fifties movie *Mon Oncle*.

A dozen stalls further down rue des Rosiers, we stumble upon a furniture shop that carries folding chairs. They're in good condition—and cheap.

"Perfect," Noah says, tucking them under his arm. "Time for a well-deserved musical lunch at Chez Louisette."

"Aren't you buying anything?"

"I was hoping to find a toy for Oscar," he says. "But no luck."

"Who's Oscar?"

"My dog."

"You mean your *imaginary* dog?" I fold my arms over my chest. "I've been to your place twice and didn't notice any pets."

His lips curl up. "I'm flattered you think I'm a guy who'd have an imaginary dog. But Oscar is real."

I arch an eyebrow.

"He's vacationing in Brittany at the moment."

My second eyebrow goes up.

"With my neighbors," Noah adds.

"Of course." I school my features into a polite expression. "Has he sent you a postcard yet? Is he enjoying himself?"

"Last time I had him on the phone, he definitely was," Noah says, unfazed.

"Glad to hear it. What else did he say? Has he done any sightseeing?"

Noah grins. "I wasn't joking, you know. Oscar uses different sounds to express his emotions and needs, and I've learned to decode the most basic ones."

"So you speak Dog."

"I understand it."

"Give me an example."

"OK." He scratches the back of his head. "Let's see. He uses a unique frustrated growl to say, *My toy is stuck under the couch and my paws are too short to get it.*"

I smile. "One more."

"A high-pitched whining sound means *I need to pee.*"

"Another one?"

"When he purrs, it roughly translates as *I like what you're doing. Please continue.*"

I tilt my head to the side. "Oscar purrs."

"Oh yes."

"And you're *sure* he's real."

"You don't believe me?"

"Err... No."

"OK." He purses his lips. "Let's bet. If Oscar doesn't exist, you get a front-row seat for the first game of the season we'll be hosting."

"And if he does?"

"You'll join me and two of my friends for a dinner at the Moose."

"What kind of place is that?"

"A Canadian sports bar."

I agree to his terms before it hits me that no matter who wins this bet, Noah and I will have to see each other again.

For the next few minutes, we follow the GPS on his phone that leads us to Chez Louisette.

"In business since 1930," Noah says in a deep TV announcer's voice as he opens the door for me.

I step inside—and tumble into a time warp.

The place is rundown as if it hasn't been refurbished since 1930, but it glitters like a Christmas tree. Tacky garlands, pom-poms, and ribbons in red and gold hang from the ceiling. Mirrored balls and chandeliers dangle between the ribbons.

As if all of that wasn't enough, gaudy string lights add to the kitschy oomph of the room, drawing the eye to the performers' corner where a pudgy old lady belts out Piaf's "*La Vie en rose*." A gentleman of matching build and age accompanies her on the accordion. Some of the diners sing along.

In the space between the tables and the bar, three or four couples dance a fast, bouncy waltz I recognize from old French movies that Mom and I watch sometimes.

I can't believe this place is real.

We sit down and order a beer for Noah, a sparkling water for me, and today's special for both, which is some kind of simmered dish.

The singer finishes "*La Vie en rose*" and moves on to the equally famous "*Non, je ne regrette rien.*"

"Do you have friends or family here in Paris?" Noah asks.

"My mom lives here."

"Are your parents separated?"

"Divorced."

"Mine, too," he says.

"Is your dad in France?"

Noah smirks. "His grave is."

"I'm sorry."

"I'm not."

My eyebrows shoot up.

"He was a nasty piece of work," Noah says.

"That's harsh."

"Why? My father was debauched, unreliable, tightfisted, and mean."

"Really? All of those things?"

"I'll give you an example. Several years after the divorce Maman needed money, so she swallowed her pride and asked him for help. He said no. So I swallowed my teenage pride and asked if he could please help her. The answer was still no."

"Was he broke?" I ask.

"Yes, but not in the usual sense of the word," he says cryptically, a grim look on his face.

My heart goes out to him. Despite my parents' divorce, I enjoyed a sheltered, happy childhood with both Mom and Dad doting on me and rich enough to get me almost anything I wanted. Noah, on the other hand, sounds like he grew up in poverty and rejected by his dad. It must've been hard for him.

"How was living on a shoestring?" I ask.

"We weren't poor," he mutters, turning away.

Great. Now I've hurt his pride.

Our food and drinks arrive, offering a much-needed distraction.

"How did you come to play water polo?" I ask, changing the topic. "Is it a popular sport in Nepal?"

His face crinkles up in a smile. "Nepalis prefer elephant polo."

"Have you played it?"

He shakes his head. "I guess I'm too French for that. Besides, I love water and swimming, and I love ball games like handball and basketball."

"You're sure tall enough for basketball."

"I did play it for a short while in middle school. But the day I tried water polo, I knew it was my sport."

The singer, who'd left the room momentarily, returns to her spot. She nods to the man on the accordion and starts crooning, "*Padam... Padam...*"

"It's my favorite Piaf song," I say.

A middle-aged man and a woman two tables to our left stand up and launch into a bouncy waltz in front of the bar.

"Isn't this dance called *la java*?" I ask Noah.

"No clue," he says. "Want to give it a try?"

I blink at him. "Can you dance it?"

"Nope. But it doesn't look too complicated to me."

The temptation is too strong, so I set my glass on the table. "I might step on your toes."

"Step away."

He offers his hand, and we head to the improvised dance floor.

As we begin our clumsy stomp and whirl, all I can think of is Noah's hand holding mine, snug and tight. His other hand settles just above the low waistline of my jeans. His palm is huge. It wraps around my hip gently, but I can sense the strength in it, and I can certainly feel its warmth through the thin fabric of my tee. My skin prickles. What's weird about this is that I find his touch... pleasant.

"What's your function on the team?" I ask to take my mind off that troubling thought.

"Goalie."

"Was that your choice?"

"It was more by chance than by choice," he says. "When I joined the team in college, my coach needed someone to man the cage. I was the biggest guy on the team and, as it turned out after a few games, a natural at blocking."

"I envy you," I say. "I've been good at most things I've tried, but I've never been a *natural* at anything."

He gives me a wink. "Keep trying things."

When the song ends and we return to our table, Noah pulls out his smartphone. "So, let's get that bet settled."

"Now?"

He nods, tapping and scrolling on his phone until he finds what he's looking for. Holding up the phone, he shows me a dozen pictures of him and his furry companion. Then he shows me a short video of him scratching the dog's throat.

Oscar tips his head back and purrs. The sound he makes is low, soft and continuous, and it's definitely saying, *Oh yeah, right there, so good.*

"All right," I say, looking up at Noah. "You win."

He grins.

"So who are these friends of yours that I'll have the honor of meeting?"

"One is Uma," he says. "My best friend. She's arriving from Nepal this weekend."

"For a visit?"

"No, for longer." He gives me a weird look I can't read. "Forever, I hope."

His last words rattle me inexplicably.

"And the other one?" I ask.

"Zach, my team captain." Noah's gaze is trained on his beer as he adds, "He's a successful businessman and an all-around great guy. Zach is looking to meet a lovely young woman… like you."

Hey-ho.

I force a smile. "That would be great."

SEVEN
Noah

I park my scooter a few blocks from Zach's house and head to his charming redbrick at the end of the street. Zach lives in Inry, a residential suburb of Paris that I'd never set foot in until Uma and I moved her things here.

She got her visa and arrived in France ten days ago.

The original plan had been that she'd stay in the Derzians' empty apartment until late August, when my kind neighbors return from Brittany. By then, she'd find a job and a room in a shared rental or in a student residence at Cité Universitaire. But Zach was eager for her to start as soon as possible. She did, and according to Zach, she hit it off with Sam immediately.

I'm happy about that, not in the least because I was the artisan of this arrangement. And it's fucking perfect any way you look at it. First of all, Uma will be able to return the grant money she believes others need more. Second, she'll be safe with Zach, whom I'd trust with my life, so Maman and I don't need to worry. Third, Zach got a huge weight off his shoulders. He can focus on the games again and start dating.

About that.

I called Sophie this morning to see if she was free on Saturday night for that dinner we'd discussed at the flea market. She said she was. I said "awesome" except awesome is the last thing I feel about it.

I keep thinking of our *la java* dance in that tacky bistro, two weeks back. We goofed around and I kept her at a safe distance from start to finish, but boy, was it hard. Just like the first time we met when I did a full salute within seconds of pinning her to the wall.

As we danced, the hand I'd placed on her hip as lightly as I could, itched to hold her harder. My fingers ached to caress her slim back. My palm burned to press into her hip so I could learn its exact curve and imprint its shape into my flesh before sliding lower to gloss her mind-blowing butt. As if that wasn't enough, the urge to crush her against my chest and claim her full mouth almost drove me to the brink of insanity.

Had the singer done one extra chorus of "*Padam... Padam...*," I might've lost control and done all of those things.

There's no denying that Sophie Bander is the worst distraction I've ever had to cope with. She draws me away from what's important. Worse, when I'm around her, my mind clouds over and I get this traitorous impression that nothing else matters. The season, Maman's work, Uma's future—all my goals and wishes pale next to my need to hold her.

What's even worse is that I doubt a night with her would quench my thirst.

Something tells me the opposite would happen. Having sex with her would make me want more sex with her, and the whole thing would spin out of control. Because that's who Sophie is. A dormant siren. A femme fatale pretending she's unexceptional. *Believing* she's unexceptional.

This... this *thing* has to be quashed before it's too late.

I ring Zach's doorbell.

Behind the door, someone stomps down the stairs.

"Let me get it! Let me get it!" Sam shouts excitedly.

A second person scurries to the door.

"OK, but you have to ask the *question* first," Uma says, laughing.

"OK! Who's there?" Sam hollers.

"It's me," I say, putting an eye to the peephole.

There's a silence. I picture Sam looking up at Uma for guidance. She says something I can't make out.

"State your first name and..." Sam commands before stalling. "...and..."

Uma says something again in a quiet voice.

"Last name," Sam shouts. "And step away from the peephole so we can see you."

"Let me help you, buddy," Uma says behind the door, lifting him so he can look through the peephole I guess.

I draw back, smile, and say loudly. "Noah. Masson."

"I remember you," Sam cries. "You're the goalie!"

The door opens, and I step in.

Ten minutes later, the three of us sit around the kitchen table. Uma hands Sam a mug filled with some unidentified beverage and makes a Nespresso shot for each of us.

"I'll be with you in a minute!" Zach calls from upstairs. "Just need to finish this conference call."

Uma prepares another Nespresso with more water—the way Zach likes it.

"So, how is everything?" I ask.

She grins and glances at Sam who's hiding his face behind his Winnie the Pooh mug. "Couldn't be better."

Sam sets his mug on the table. "Daddy's going to the lions tomorrow, and I'm staying with Uma for two days, and we'll watch *Lilo and Stitch* and *Leroy and Stitch*."

I turn to Uma.

"Zach is going on a two-day business trip to Lyon," she explains, wiping Sam's mouth. "So, yeah, it's going to be a late night for us with Sam's favorite movies."

"Totally unfair," Zach says, walking in and sitting next to Sam. "I love that cartoon just as much as you do."

"You can join us next time," Sam says magnanimously.

Zach gives his shoulder a light squeeze. "Thanks, man."

When the boy runs away to play with his electric train, a deep crease appears between Zach's eyebrows. "I'm still nervous about going away for two days."

Uma hands him his cup. "You shouldn't be."

"You started only a week ago, and already I'm leaving you alone with him," Zach says, shaking his head.

"It's just one night." Uma sits down next to me. "Besides, you had no choice."

Zach turns to me. "I was hoping Colette would rise to the occasion for once... but that didn't happen."

I smirk as I picture Sam's mother serving Zach her standard response. Had Zach listened to her, Sam would be somebody else's responsibility now. But Zach *chose* to keep him, well aware of the boy's condition, so now Sam is Zach's problem. Not hers.

My teammate gives Uma an apologetic look. "Just say the word, and I'll cancel the trip."

"I know exactly what to do if Sam has a seizure. You should stop fretting." She stares into his eyes. "This trip is super important for your business, right?"

Zach nods. "It is. Otherwise, I wouldn't even consider going."

She shrugs.

"Uma's right," I say to Zach. "Stop fretting. You're leaving your boy in capable hands."

I mean it, too. Uma is the most dependable person in the world. She's kind, gentle, competent, and always in control. The kind of person I'd entrust with my life… and with my kid's life, if I have a kid one day.

Maman is right—she's perfect. It's humbling that a woman like that has feelings for me.

"Hey," Zach turns to me. "I never properly thanked you for arranging the outing next Saturday. Sophie sounds exactly like someone I'd want to date."

I shrug dismissively. "You'll thank me later if everything goes well. Did you find a solution for Sam?"

"I can babysit him," Uma offers.

"No way. You're coming with us." Zach gives her a wink. "Noah here would be *very* disappointed if you didn't."

"But what about Sam?" she asks.

Zach grins triumphantly. "Mathilde has agreed to come over for the evening."

"Cool." I stand up. "Thanks for the coffee, Uma."

She smiles. "Anytime."

"Will you be at the morning practice tomorrow?" I ask Zach.

He nods. "My train to *the lions* leaves at one fifteen."

* * *

When I get home, there's a letter in my mailbox. The handwriting on the envelope is Diane's.

Fantastic.

Yet another missive from my unwanted sister-in-law, who appears to be even more pigheaded than my brothers are in her refusal to let me be.

I plop onto the couch, tear the envelope open, and retrieve a sheet of paper. She's slipped in a few pictures, too, as per her habit. I set the photos aside and read the letter.

Dear Noah,

Sebastian, baby Tanguy, and I are spending another wonderful weekend at your estate. Take a look at the photos I enclosed. What do you think of the park? And isn't the castle absolutely gorgeous? The wild grapevine on the façade is so pretty against the old stones, you'd think I photoshopped it. (Just in case you do, please note I am not *that kind of girl).*

You should come and see it with your own eyes.

Oh, I will—sooner than you might expect.

Just so you know, I made several dozen large prints of that grapevine. They are framed and stacked in the storage room. They might come in handy should you choose to revamp the interior when you do the renovations, which are badly needed.

Pff. As if I cared.

Believe me, I'm not exaggerating. Chateau d'Arcy is falling apart. Given the thickness of its walls, the structure is in no danger, but the rest... If you set foot inside, I'm sure your heart will bleed. I tried to convince Seb to fix the worst of it, but he says it's not our place. He says he'll be happy to fund the works, so you won't have to deplete your trust fund for that, but you should take charge.

Do you think you could do that?

Hugs,
Diane

I lay the letter on the coffee table and lean back, clasping my hands behind my head. This note will go unanswered just like all of Diane's previous letters.

She seems to be a good girl. What a shame she had to ruin her life by marrying Seb, a.k.a. His Pompous Ass, Excellency Count Sebastian d'Arcy du Grand-Thouars de Saint-Maurice. My friendly sister-in-law is in for a lot of heartache the day she finally opens her eyes and faces the bitter truth.

Beneath the veneer of respectability, the country's oldest, richest, and most envied family has no honor The way my late father and Seb treated Maman with Raphael's tacit consent is ugly. I'll never forgive them for that. My older brothers are unworthy of the riches they own.

If only my *Papa chéri* hadn't made a will!

Had he kicked the bucket without leaving one, his estate would've been divided equally between his three sons, according to French inheritance laws. Nothing for Maman, of course, whom he'd conveniently divorced.

But he did leave a will, and I can't legally dispose of my share until I'm twenty-seven.

Guess what? I'm turning twenty-seven in six weeks' time.

I feel a prick of conscience. It has nothing to do with my plans for the estate. But it has to do with how my cryptic answers might've led Sophie to believe I'd starved in Nepal.

When I told her Papa had refused to help Maman, I failed to mention that the money she was asking for wasn't for food or shelter. She needed a half million dollars for her foundation. The initial endowment having dried up and no new sponsors forthcoming, Maman's life's achievement was going down the drain.

But she and I were doing fine on alimony. More than fine. Compared to local standards, we were rich.

So why did I let Sophie think otherwise?

I guess it was the only way to stop her from asking more questions. She's my landlady, for Christ's sake—not my friend like Uma and Zach. She'll be gone by Christmas. There's no reason why I should share with her the fucked-up story of my life.

No reason at all.

EIGHT
Sophie

The first thing I see as we enter the Moose is a rustic stone wall behind the bar with a couple of flat screens tuned to hockey.

"How very North American," Uma says with a smile. "Not that I've been to North America, but that's exactly how I imagined a sports bar somewhere in Seattle."

"This one is more Montreal than Seattle," Zach says.

The place is lit by the dim glow of ceiling spots and at least a dozen wall-mounted flat-screen TVs. Polished wood and moose antlers dominate the decor.

The four of us had met by the statue of Danton at Odéon, which is spitting distance from here. I'd ridden the *métro* from work, Uma and Zach had arrived in his car, and Noah on his scooter.

Now that it stays warm after dusk, I revel in the pleasant coolness of this bar.

We make our way to the sitting area and pick one of the two vacant tables.

To our left, a large boisterous group is having a lively conversation in Quebecois French so thick you could slice it with a knife.

I jerk my chin in their direction. "Looks like we've found the place where Canadian tourists come to chill after a hard day's sightseeing."

"But that's a good sign, right?" Uma says. "Canadians wouldn't come here if this place wasn't authentic."

Noah smiles. "The main reason they come here is that there aren't a lot of sports bars in Paris."

Zach nods. "And even fewer where you can watch the Super Bowl, Stanley Cup and NBA playoffs in real time."

"And eat a decent poutine," Noah adds.

Zach raises his index finger. "*Pootseen*, please, if you want to sound Quebecois."

"What's a *Pootseen*?" I ask.

Noah and Zach exchange a meaningful glance.

"You'll discover soon enough," Noah says.

I think he was warning me, and I burst out laughing at his amusing air of mystery.

"Ladies." Zach looks from Uma to me and then to Noah. "Gentleman. Do I have everyone's permission to order your food and drinks?"

I narrow my eyes. "Depends on what you're ordering."

"You allergic to anything?" he asks.

I shake my head.

"Relax, Sophie," Noah touches my hand. "Nobody's treating you to fried crickets. We'll have Moosehead—a Canadian beer—and poutine."

I sigh. "Beer is fine. It's poutine that I'm worried about."

"Hang on." Uma rummages through her tote bag, muttering, "He used to do this all the time when we were kids—asking if I'd like a profiterole or a bit of *aligot* or a slice of *tatin*, and I had to say yes or no before he'd tell me what those things were."

"Did I ever trick you into eating something you hated?" Noah asks her.

"That's not the point." She pulls out a smartphone. "Ta-da! Don't you love modern technology? No more surprises. We're going to find out what poutine is in a moment."

Zach waves a server over, while Uma fumbles with her phone.

"Found it," she announces a few seconds later and begins to read out loud.

> Poutine was invented in Quebec under mysterious circumstances and in an undisclosed location sixty years ago. It has since become Canada's national dish. The classic poutine ("*la classique*") is made from hand-cut French fries topped with cheese curds (called *crottes de fromage* by locals, which means "cheese poop") and with hot brown gravy called *velouté*. Greasy and calorie rich, poutine is the ultimate comfort food.

Uma drops her phone back into her handbag and grins. "Sounds yummy."

Does she mean it?

I peer at her face and conclude to my horror that she does.

If I were a blunt kind of girl, I would've told these people what poutine sounded like from a health-conscious Floridian's perspective. It sounded like love handles, pimples, and a heart attack.

Zach turns to the waiter. "We'll have four Mooseheads and four classic poutines."

"Awesome." I bare my teeth. "Right up my alley. Can't wait."

I wonder if any of them can hear the sarcasm in my voice.

Noah hems before shifting his gaze from me to one of the TV screens. His lips are twitching.

Five minute later the server brings our frosty beers and steaming plates.

I stare at the huge serving of fries and rubbery cheese curds smothered in gravy. "This doesn't look very… appetizing."

"Don't be afraid to say it looks like shit," Noah says.

"The proof of the pudding isn't in looking pretty," Zach says. "It's in the eating."

With the fuck-it-all determination of a kamikaze pilot, I pick up my fork and knife. "All right, let's eat."

The cheese curds squeak in my mouth as I chew.

"I recommend you wash it down with beer," Noah says, his eyes riveted to my mouth. "It'll help your palate handle the shock."

Uma turns to me. "Isn't this the kind of food you're used to?"

I shake my head. "In Key West, we have lots of options to choose from. You can eat Cuban or vegetarian or French or... whatever. I usually go for French as I'm used to it."

"Sophie's mom is French," Noah says.

"That explains it." Zach gives me a bright smile. "I was wondering why your French was so good— barely a hint of an accent."

I acknowledge his compliment with a polite smile.

"What kind of place is Key West?" Noah asks.

"In one word?" I chew on my lower lip, thinking. "Relaxed. You'd like it."

"Tell me more." His eyes are on my mouth again.

Is that why I keep biting my lip?

I'm not in the habit of doing that—actually, I *never* do that. But there's something highly addictive in the way he stares at my mouth. The heat of his gaze makes me want to encourage him, makes me hungry for more.

Get a grip, Sophie.

I shrug. "In a nutshell—we have a tropical climate, the best beaches and sunsets, occasional hurricanes, and hordes of tourists on Duval Street." Winking, I add, "As well as lovely wood houses for sale via my dad's agency. Should anyone be interested."

An hour later, Zach settles the bill, and I use the occasion to study his face. The man is certainly good-looking. He's been the perfect gentleman throughout the dinner. So, why am I hoping Noah will offer me a ride home?

"Can I offer you a lift?" Zach asks me, standing up.

"I live in the 18th," I say. "You and Uma would have to make a huge detour and lose an hour, if not more."

This would be Noah's cue to jump in and offer that ride.

But he doesn't. He studies his shoes.

Uma turns to Zach. "Why don't I take the *métro* so that we don't delay Mathilde, and you take Sophie home?"

"I'll give you a lift," Noah says to Uma. "It'll be faster."

Shoot.

Inside Zach's Beamer, he makes small talk and I nod as we drive north through the quiet city bathed in the soft light from windows and street lamps. The stereo streams jazzy French music. Add that to the air-conditioning and Zach's deep, masculine bass, and this *should* be a very pleasant ride. Romantic, even.

But it's confusion, not romance, that fills my mind right now.

My thoughts return to the Moose. The food sucked, but I truly enjoyed the company. Uma was totally sweet. Zach was gracious. Noah was... Noah. We ate, drank, joked, and pretended our "dinner among friends" wasn't really a double date, and we weren't really two couples in the making.

Couple Number 1—Uma and Noah, childhood besties teetering between friendship and something more.

Couple Number 2—Zach and I testing the waters to see if we click.

Do we click? I guess so.

In addition to being gorgeous, Zach is also a wealthy go-getter interested in a relationship. Unlike Noah.

Besides, he fits Dad's idea of a perfect catch to a T.

If I am to give the whole dating thing another shot and go out with someone while I'm in Paris, it should be him. In fact, I can't find a single reason why we shouldn't date.

My mind conjures up an image of Uma and Noah huddled together on his scooter.

It's decided.

If Zach asks me out, I'll say yes.

NINE
Noah

I'm headed to the Parc des Buttes-Chaumont with a blanket, a pillow, an ultralight bivvy tent, and a cold beer stuffed into my duffel when my phone beeps.

It's a text from Sophie.

Are you asleep? I wanted to ask you a quick question, but it can certainly wait until tomorrow. Sophie

I tap a quick reply.

Awake. Shoot.

My curiosity piqued, I keep looking at the screen to read her reply as soon as it arrives. But, instead of beeping, my phone rings.

"Sorry for calling you this late," Sophie says. "I'd expected you'd be in bed already."

It hits me how much I like the sound of her voice. Feminine, velvety, sexy as hell. Even the most innocuous thing she says feels like a caress. I could listen to her say innocuous—and not so innocuous—things all day.

"Ten is a little early even for us larky athletes," I say. "Not to mention it's impossible to sleep in this heat."

"Tell me about it!" She lets out a sigh. "Why is it that no one has AC in Paris?"

"Because we don't believe global warming is real."

"Hmm." She doesn't sound convinced.

"Or maybe because we don't get heat waves every year, and they don't last long, so we hesitate to fork over several thousand euros on AC."

"That sounds more like the French," she says, a smile in her voice. "So what do you do to be able to sleep?"

"By 'you' are you referring to the French as a nation or me, Noah Masson, as a person?"

There's a brief pause before she replies. "You as a person."

"Tonight, I'm trying my luck outdoors. The town hall has opened several parks for overnight camping, so I'll be bivouacking in Buttes-Chaumont. I'm heading there as we speak."

"I'm not far from there myself," she says. "My boss and I were showing an apartment nearby, and then had a couple of drinks, so I'm still in the hood."

"Your boss takes you out for drinks," I say pointedly before I can stop myself. "How kind of him."

Shit.

That was totally uncalled for. The kind of relationship Sophie has with her boss is none of my business. She's my landlady, not my girlfriend.

"It *is* very kind of *her*," Sophie says. "I couldn't dream of a better boss for my first paid internship."

I wish I could bang my head against something right now, hard. "Of course. That comment was way too macho, even for me. I'm really sorry."

"I forgive you," she says, her voice returning to velvety.

My shoulders sag with relief. "You said you had a question."

"I did."

"I'm listening."

"Err… Do you mind if I meet you in the park and I ask in person? I promise it won't take long."

Every nerve ending in my body perks up at "meet you" and dances a little jig at "in person." My pulse kicks into high gear and my cock stirs in my pants.

"It's about Zach," she says.

Oh.

Of course. Now that she's met him—and, no doubt, *liked* him—she wants to know more about him. What did I expect?

"Sure," I say, trying to sound pleased. "Can you be at the main entrance on the corner of Botzaris and Simon-Bolivar in ten minutes?"

"Fifteen."

"Great. See you there."

Thirty minutes later, we're sitting next to each other—me cross-legged and Sophie hugging her knees—on the blanket I've spread under a tree. She's wearing a flowy summer dress with a hem that bares her lithe calves and part of her thighs. My gaze travels down to her feet. They're clad in sandals with sexy straps that crisscross and snake around her slim ankles. Her toenails are painted dark red.

They are the most beautiful feet I've ever laid eyes on.

My chest clenches with longing.

Cut the crap, Noah.

That's way too much appreciation for a woman you're trying to set up with a friend.

Peeling my gaze off her, I look around. At least a hundred couples, groups, and individuals have set camp on the vast lawn, prepping for a night under the stars.

I pull the beer out of my bag and open it. "Want some? We better drink it while it's still cold."

"Thank you." She takes a swig and gives the can back. "That felt good."

Lifting the can to my mouth, I wonder if I'll taste Sophie. I wonder what her lush, delicious-looking lips taste like. What her perfect skin tastes like. What her little—

"How well do you know Zach?" she asks.

Talk about cold showers.

On the other hand, I needed this.

"Pretty well. We've been on the same team almost two years now."

"He seems like a nice guy."

"He is." I nod. "Better than nice. He's awesome."

"How come he's raising his kid alone?"

"Zach's ex-girlfriend didn't want the burden of a child with a chronic health condition."

"Oh."

"Sam's epilepsy is manageable," I add quickly. "He'll go to school next year like other kids his age. When he grows up, he can live a normal life, provided he takes his meds."

She nods.

"Look," I say. "I totally get it if you hesitate because of that, but you shouldn't."

"That's not why I—"

"Besides," I add before she can finish. "You can date Zach without getting involved with his kid. Sam has two nannies and an adoring dad to take care of him."

She frowns. "That's not why I hesitate. It's just… I'm not sure I should start a relationship or even date, when I know I'm going back home in December."

"So what?" I shrug. "Why not have some fun while you're in Paris?"

"It's… complicated."

"Try me."

"You really want to hear it?"

I nod.

She snatches the beer from me, takes a good swig, and hands it back to me. "I'm frigid."

You? No way.

"Are you sure?" I ask.

She nods. "I've dated three different men, had sex with each of them, and never felt anything."

I study her face.

"Worse," she says. "I actually did feel something—pain and discomfort."

My hand touches her cheek before my brain can step in. "I'm sorry."

She doesn't jerk away.

"Now that I've adjusted my expectations," she says, running her hands down her shins, "I find lots of advantages to my condition."

My gaze follows her fingers that are wrapped around her ankles now. "Like what?"

"No distractions, no heartbreaks, no ill-matched boyfriends to be ashamed of later."

"I see."

The hell I do.

What I really see right now in the soft yellowish light of the nearby streetlamp has nothing to do with ill-matched boyfriends. My world is focused on Sophie's slim ankles, the breathtaking arch of her soles and her long, callus-free toes.

Did I suddenly become a foot fetishist?

"Besides," she says. "I can be rational about picking my future life partner, and make Dad happy by choosing a man who meets his criteria."

"Which are?"

"Successful, ambitious, and gallant." She gives me a funny look. "Someone like Zach."

I glance up at her face. "Your dad has a lot of common sense."

"Gobs of it."

"He wants what's best for you."

"Absolutely."

"But… don't you ever wonder if there's a man out there who'd make you feel things that aren't pain or discomfort?"

"I do, but then I remind myself this is the way I'm wired." She sighs. "It would be foolish to wait for some fairy-tale prince whose kiss would wake me up from my sleep."

"You tried to have sex three times, right?" I cock my head.

She nods.

"That's not *a lot*."

She says nothing.

"Three disappointments aren't enough to conclude that's the way you're *wired*."

Sophie studies a tiny bug traveling down her hand.

"Tell me about each of those times," I say.

"I can't." She shifts her position. "Anyway, I should get going."

I glance at my watch. "It'll be midnight soon. I don't like the idea of you alone on the deserted streets."

"What's the alternative?"

I should offer to call her a cab. "Stay here."

"In the park?" She furrows her brow.

I point at my bivvy. "You'll be safer with me here than on the *métro*."

She peers at me.

I stare back, praying she'll say yes.

Because if she says no, I'm going to pack up and take the *métro* to the 18th with her, then try to catch the last train or hoof it back here. There's no way I'm saying good-bye now. I need a little more of Sophie tonight.

Please say yes.

She picks up the beer can and gulps down the rest of the liquid. "Are there any restrooms in this park?"

Fingers crossed this means yes.

"There's a toilet right there." I point toward a one-story building to our left.

She stands up. "I'll be back."

When she returns a few minutes later, I'm lying on my back with my knees bent and hands clasped under my head.

She lies down next to me, mirroring my position. "You'd expect to see more stars."

"This is plenty for Paris."

We stare at the night sky for a few minutes.

"My first time was with a classmate," she says. "We were sixteen. We were both of us so inept it's a small miracle we actually managed to get rid of our virginity."

I turn to look at her face. She's wincing.

"Not a happy memory, huh?"

She shakes her head. "I was *so* not ready."

"Did you let him near you again?"

"Nope. I broke up with him immediately. He cried."

"What about the second time?"

"The second boyfriend…" She's silent for a long moment. "Sophomore year. I didn't want to rush things, and he said he respected that. So we abstained for a while. And then…"

She expels her breath in a slow hiss.

"And then?"

"I agreed to have sex with him. I thought I liked him. He'd been perfectly likable before he stripped and started touching me." Her words come out fast and angry. "And suddenly, he was repulsive. His smell, his touch, his kisses…"

She releases another long breath.

I turn my head toward her. Sophie's jaw is set, her nostrils flaring, as she's reliving that situation.

"Did—" I begin to form my question.

"The third one," she says with an exaggerated nonchalance, "was the most pathetic experience of all. I was so not into it during foreplay that I went to the bathroom while he was looking for a condom, locked the door, and asked him to leave."

"Ouch." I say. "I wouldn't want to be in that guy's shoes."

She shrugs. "So I figured sex was overrated."

"Do you think you might be into women?"

"No. Definitely not."

"Good," I say.

"Why?"

"Because that gorgeous body of yours was made to be touched by a man."

She smirks. "Here comes the macho again!"

But she's wrong. My comment had nothing to do with machismo. What I meant by "a man" wasn't abstract. The man I had in mind was specific and concrete with a birth name he'd chosen to discard years ago, and a straining cock he's choosing to ignore right now.

This man.

TEN
Sophie

For a moment Noah's eyes burn into mine, intense. He shifts closer to me, ever so slightly, and opens his mouth as if he's about to say something.

And then he blinks and looks away.

When he turns back to me a few seconds later, his expression is unreadable.

"I'm sorry," he says. "Feel free to gag me before I make another highly inappropriate comment."

I pull a face. "Gagging is so *Fifty Shades*. How about duct tape?"

"Really?" He frowns and shrugs. "If that's what floats your boat..."

"Did you pack any, by chance?"

He shakes his head.

I sigh. "In that case, there's only one thing left to do."

He gives me a quizzical look.

"Sleep."

"Good idea." He jumps up. "I'm going to open the bivvy and move the blanket inside, if you don't mind."

I stand up, too. "Won't we be too warm inside?"

"Don't worry." He unfolds the contraption which turns out to be a narrow one-person tent. "See the mesh on the sides? Keeps bugs out but lets air in."

I tip my head back and close my eyes hoping for a night breeze, but the air is as still and sultry as it was at midday.

"Not sure we want *this* air in," I say.

"The temperature will drop soon."

Opening my eyes, I glance at the bivvy. "It's going to be tight in there."

"Are you an aggressive sleeper?"

I smile. "I don't jump, kick, or snore in my sleep if that's what you mean."

"Me neither." Noah throws a small pillow into the bivvy. "We'll be fine."

He steps out of his flip-flops and climbs inside.

I remove my sandals. This is crazy. As in, *crazy exciting.*

When I crawl in, Noah has moved as far to the left as the tent allows, leaving me half of the available space and the whole pillow.

I turn to him, propping myself up. "Can you sleep without a pillow?"

He glances at it and then at me as if considering his options. "You're right. I'll need something."

Sitting up, he pulls off his T-shirt, folds it, and lies back down, tucking it under his head.

My lips part as I take in the glorious triangle of his torso.

Frigid or not, all that smooth, hard, chiseled *manliness*—this close—makes an impression.

Stop ogling his chest, Sophie!

I look at his hands instead. "They're big."

Shoot. Did I just say that out loud?

"You mean my hands?" he asks.

"Uh-huh."

He lifts his right hand and splays his fingers. "Having big hands is an asset for a water polo goalie. As is a large body size, arm span, speed of reaction, and a firm grip."

A firm grip. I swallow.

"Reaction speed is probably the most important feature," Noah says. "A shorter goalie who's explosive will get into the corners faster and block better than a big goalie who's slow."

"So, the ideal is a big explosive goalie, right?"

"Right."

I give him a wink. "Which is where you come in."

He smiles, blushing a little.

Aww. Could this man get any sweeter? I need a joke before my heart melts into a sticky mess. Any dumb crack will do.

"Don't take it the wrong way," I say, "but water polo players look a little funny."

"Funny how?"

"You know, with those bonnets tied neatly under your chins. And your chests are shaved…"

"It's to reduce drag and increase speed."

"Of course. But still…" I give him a sly smile. "It does reinforce the look."

"What look?"

My gaze flicking to his nipples, I mutter, "Baby look."

"Really?"

"Come on," I nudge him. "Can you deny that water polo players look like babies? Huge, muscular, testosterone-fueled babies."

"Sophie." He arches an eyebrow in fake admonishment. "That was sexist and highly inappropriate."

I drop my head to my chest to show I regret my words. Which I don't. Not for a second.

"What's the word for a macho woman?" he asks.

"Hmm… Man-eater?"

He shakes his head.

"Femdom?" I try again.

"Warmer, but still off the mark."

"Butch?"

He sighs. "I'll have to write a letter to the Académie Française urging them to coin a word for women like you."

"Knock yourself out," I say.

"I'm going to propose *femcho*."

I snort. "That sounds perfectly ridiculous. Makes me think of that fluffy poncho I bought a few years back and never dared to wear."

"Hmm…" He rubs his chin, drawing my attention to the bulging muscles of his upper arm.

"Femcho accusations aside, how do you guys get so fit?" I ask.

He smiles. "We swim at least 2,000 meters during each workout, lift weights for body strength, and stretch for flexibility. Um… what else? We practice shooting and treading water until our arms and legs fall off. You know, the usual 'testosterone-fueled baby' stuff."

If I look at his mouth or his torso a second longer, I might squeal. Or make another inane comment. Or reach over and touch him.

Truth is, I have no idea what I might do because I've never felt this way before.

"Right." I turn away from Noah. "Do you think this light will go off at some point? I find it hard to fall asleep unless it's completely dark."

"Don't know," he says. "Never slept in a park before."

"I need to be at the office early. Do you mind if I set my phone alarm to seven thirty?"

"Mine is set to seven," he says. "I don't want to be late for the morning practice."

"Good night."

"Sweet dreams."

I breathe in the faint scent of Noah's aftershave and shut my eyes. The lawn where we're camping is a lot quieter now than it was half an hour ago, with almost everyone around us having crept into their tents and sleeping bags. I should be able to fall asleep easily.

Fifteen minutes later, I turn toward Noah again.

He's still flat on his back with his eyes wide open.

"The mesh on the other side lets too much light in," I say to justify my change of position.

He turns on his side to face me, folds his right arm under his head, and places his left hand between us, a bare inch from my breasts.

The heat coming off him and the scent of his skin—a touch of aftershave and a lot of Noah—messes with my brain. They take my thoughts and my senses to a place that's entirely new to me. I feel like I was beamed into a rain forest. It's hot, lush and full of surprises.

And scary.

"There's this theory in quantum physics," I say, scrambling to find my bearings.

He gives a crooked smile. "My fair landlady is a closet geek?"

"Not at all." I chuckle. "I just stumbled upon an article a few years back, and it stayed with me."

"What's it about?"

"The mechanics of touch," I say. "According to quantum physics, you can never really touch anything."

"What do you mean?"

"Everything is composed of tiny particles, right?"

He nods.

"Particles repel other particles of the same kind," I say. "For example, when you sit in a chair, you're actually hovering above it."

He furrows his brow. "Then why did my ass always feel sore after sitting in a chair through a double period at school?"

"If I remember correctly," I say with a smile, "it's because the waves you generate overlap with the chair's waves, and your brain misinterprets it as touching."

"So if I do *this*,"—he puts his hand on my hip—"I'm not actually touching you. Is that what you're saying?"

I swallow, trying to keep the smile on my face. "Yes."

He lets his fingers and the ball of his palm gently sink into my flesh without pressing or rubbing. With every second that passes, I feel my body respond to his hand hug. Through the thin silk of my dress, my skin tingles, and the flesh under his hand begins to burn.

Suddenly, the mischievous gleam in his eyes gives way to an entirely different expression.

My smile slips, too.

What's happening to me?

How did I go from pondering if I should date Zach earlier this evening to wondering which direction Noah will move his hand—up to cup my breast or down to stroke my thigh. And how my body would react to it. And whether my need for him to do that is bigger than my fear.

What if this excitement I'm feeling isn't real and has nothing to do with a normal arousal a normal woman would feel? What if it's just wishful thinking? I may believe I'm aroused, but what will happen when he touches me more intimately? Will the illusion melt into thin air? Will my body stiffen with revulsion, just like it's done before?

The ironic truth is I'd be less anxious if I felt nothing—I'd know what to expect.

But with my body acting so out of character, setting my expectations high and giving me hope, it's just too scary.

"I don't think I'm ready for this," I say, butterflies in my stomach.

He doesn't respond for the longest moment with his hand on my waist and his eyes riveted to mine.

"That's OK," he finally says. "We should try to get some sleep."

Nodding with relief, I turn my back to Noah and push the pillow to the middle, offering him half of it. "I doubt it's comfortable sleeping on a folded tee."

He draws closer, laying his head on the pillow. I feel his warm breath on the back of my neck.

"Do you mind if I put my hand back where it was?" he asks.

"Suit yourself."

His hand returns to my waist and slides over to my belly. Should I tell him off for taking more than he was given? While I'm mulling over that question, he shifts, wrapping his entire arm around me and pulling me closer.

This is so much more than the authorized hand-on-waist that I lose my tongue momentarily.

Next thing I know he's pressing his chest against my back and snaking a leg over my thigh.

"Good night, Sophie," he says, his voice hoarse.

Recovering from my stupor, I finally move. But, instead of drawing away, I arch my body into him, looking for an additional point of contact.

There it is! The hard ridge I'd felt the day we first met when he'd tackled me in his kitchen. I love its length and thickness and the way it nestles against my derriere.

How shocking.

How totally inexplicable and sexy.

"Good night," I rasp, barely recognizing my voice.

What does the quantum theory have to say about this, I wonder? For years, it's been my handy justification for not reacting to a man's touch. Except I'm reacting all right to Noah's. Let's face it—I may not be as frigid as I thought.

How else can I explain that at the ripe age of twenty-four, and against all expectations, Princess Sophie was suddenly roused from her sexuality-free slumber?

I wish my savior were Zach the Successful Entrepreneur.

Or—even better—some hotshot business shark in Florida. But instead, it's Delivery Man Noah... *Damn!* Why did I have to be awakened by a guy who, on top of having neither money nor ambition, possibly nurtures a longtime crush on his childhood bestie?

How fucking ironic is that?

ELEVEN
Noah

Sophie and I head to my place, our feet sinking into the heat-softened asphalt with every step. If I focus on it, it looks as if it's steaming. Just like my brain.

The plan is to drop in, take a quick shower, swallow some coffee and toasts, and jump on my scooter. I'll give her a lift to her office and hightail it to the swimming pool.

We haven't uttered a word that wasn't *practical* since we woke up this morning.

Last night was… I don't even know what it was.

We drank a can of beer. Neglected to admire the stars. Chatted. Connected.

She flirted with me… I think.

I lusted after her, touched her, hugged her.

She let me.

But she wasn't ready for more. She suspects she's frigid.

As we lay down in the bivvy, I breathed in her head-turning scent and struggled to appease a raging hard-on. Finally, in the wee hours of the morning, I fell asleep, still clutching Sophie to my chest.

I woke up to the alarm on my phone, a little dizzy—and very confused.

My mind is still muddled. The sticky heat that hasn't abated in weeks isn't helping. I can't wait to climb into the shower and let a cold jet lower my body temperature a notch. Perhaps it will cool my brain, too.

I glance at Sophie, but she won't look at me. She's eyeing an ice cream stand instead with an expression of desperate longing on her lovely face.

Halting in front of it, I touch her arm. "Ice cream break?"

She beams.

"What flavor for *Mademoiselle*?" the vendor asks.

"Strawberry cheesecake and chocolate chip cookie, please." Sophie opens her purse.

I beat her to it, placing a tenner onto the counter.

She scowls at me.

I scowl back.

She closes her purse and takes her cone from the vendor.

"Aren't you having one?" she asks me.

"I lost my sweet tooth with my milk teeth," I say, collecting the change.

"You should've let me pay," she says as we march away. "Five euros for two scoops is a ripoff."

"I delivered four pepperonis in the 6th yesterday, and the guy tipped me five euros." I shrug. "Easy come, easy go."

"Still…" She gives the frozen treat an enthusiastic lick. "So good. And exactly what I needed right now."

Watching her tongue flick in and out of her mouth, I struggle not to dwell on what *I* need right now.

"I hope the heat lets up by Saturday," I say to take my mind off those dangerous thoughts. "The Derzians are coming back with my dog, and I wouldn't want the poor thing to suffer the way he did before they left."

"Is he very furry?" she asks, turning to me.

"Not very, but enough to have a harder time than humans coping with the heat."

She gives me a sympathetic smile. "It's nice of your neighbors to take care of your dog like that."

I nod. "They're the best. Of course, it helps that Oscar and their own dog, Cannelle, get along like gangbusters, but still. The Derzians have been incredibly kind to Oscar and me ever since I moved into the apartment."

"Do they have children of their own?"

"A grown son and a daughter, both living abroad with their spouses and kids," I say. "The son is in China and the daughter in the US."

"You know where?"

"LA."

"Don't your neighbors want to move closer to at least one of their kids and grandchildren?" she asks. "Or are they such hardcore Parisians it would take a bubonic plague epidemic to get them to resettle?"

I chuckle. "As it happens, they *are* hardcore Parisians, even though they weren't born here. They're Armenians from Lebanon."

"Oh?"

I nod as we stop at the traffic light. "They visited Paris as tourists in the seventies and fell in love with the city. When war broke out in Lebanon and they fled, Paris was an obvious destination."

"They must've had a hard time rebuilding their lives from scratch in a foreign country."

"Apparently, it was easier than they'd expected," I say as we turn onto my street. "They made friends, found jobs, and felt at home within a month of their arrival. *Madame* Derzian is convinced the love they have for the city is mutual."

Sophie smiles. "So she believes Paris fell in love with them, eh? Just like that, at first sight?"

"Yep," I say. "Not immigration authorities, though."

She raises her eyebrows.

"When the Derzians applied for a residency permit, an immigration official said, 'You must understand—we can't allow everyone who loves Paris to stay here. If we did, we'd have to make room for at least a billion people. You should return to your home country.' "

"What did the Derzians do?" Sophie asks.

"They momentarily *forgot* they spoke fluent French like many Lebanese."

"And?"

"*Monsieur* Derzian spread his arms and said, 'Pardon. No speak French. Speak Armenian.' " I raise my hands, palms up, imitating *Monsieur* Derzian's gesture and accent. "The official didn't speak Armenian, which gave the Derzians an excuse to ignore his instruction and stay put."

She laughs. "How convenient! So your wonderful neighbors are illegal aliens?"

"Not anymore," I say. "They reapplied a few years later and were granted a residency permit."

We enter my building and rush up the stairs to my apartment. Which, technically, is Sophie's. Just another bit of weirdness she's brought into my life.

I hand her a clean towel and a new toothbrush. While she showers, I brew some coffee.

She comes out of the bathroom less than ten minutes later, smelling of my shower gel. "Your turn."

When I return to the kitchen, having washed and changed into clean clothes, Sophie has toasted two slices of bread.

I pour both of us some java.

She takes her cup from me and points to my toast. "Wasn't sure how you like it."

"With butter," I say, opening the fridge. "You?"

"Peanut butter and jelly."

I make a face. "Really?"

"I know," she says. "It's an affront to good—that is to say, French—taste. But it's stronger than me."

"I'm afraid I don't have either of those foods."

"No problem," she says. "I'll channel my French half and eat my toast with regular butter. We have to go in a few minutes, anyway."

I glance at my watch and nod.

"About last night," Sophie says, as I drink my coffee.

I set the cup on the table and stare at her.

"I feel guilty." She looks downward. "I sort of led you on and left you hanging."

"I don't—"

"I just want you to know I wasn't playing or anything." She glances at me and looks down again. "I did enjoy being touched by you. It's just… I don't know if I can handle another disappointment if it turns out that I am hopelessly frigid, after all."

"Sophie Bander," I say in a know-it-all teacher's voice. "You are *not* frigid."

"How can you be sure?"

"Because you want me."

She looks up at me again.

I hold her gaze.

She mustn't suspect how much I'm gambling here.

Both of my claims—that she isn't frigid and that she wants me—are based on a gut feeling, not certitude. Especially the latter one. For all I know, it's Zach she'd rather hook up with. He'll probably take her to dinner one of these days, charm her, date her, pamper her, and marry while the iron is hot.

"You know what?" she says at length, her gaze still locked with mine. "I think you're right. It does look like I want you."

I suck in a sharp breath.

She tilts her head to the side. "So what are you going to do about it, Noah Masson?"

TWELVE
Sophie

I get off the *métro* and march toward Parc de la Villette where I am to finally meet Noah's dog, Oscar.

We'll walk around the park—seeing as dogs aren't allowed inside—and head to Noah's for a bite and chilled *rosé*.

I didn't take my backpack as I have no intention of sleeping over even if it's Friday night. Véronique has tasked me with showing an apartment at ten tomorrow morning, all by myself. This fills me with a ridiculous amount of pride... and anxiety. I've spent the last two evenings revising my notes about the apartment and the neighborhood and rereading the survey reports. When I get home tonight, I'll go through everything once again, and one last time tomorrow morning before I meet with the clients.

There's a second reason I'm seeing Noah this evening, and it makes me even jitterier than tomorrow's baptism of fire.

Lovemaking.

It's always so smooth and easy in movies, but it's been the opposite in my personal experience. Just thinking about doing it again makes my hands clammy.

I'll think about Oscar instead.

Even though I'm a cat person and have no clue how to act around a dog, meeting Oscar doesn't stress me at all. Probably because Noah has told me his dog is part feline.

Yesterday afternoon right after I hung up with my soon-to-be lover, Zach texted me that he'd had fun at the Moose and we should get together again sometime.

I replied:

Definitely, as friends.

He texted:

Sure, no problem.

In the evening, I went to Mom's and told her about Zach and Noah, fully expecting a rant on my lack of common sense. Instead, she declared that Noah sounded like the kind of guy I needed.

Mom's eccentric like that.

She never sees the world the way Dad and I do.

To any rational observer, *Zach* is the kind of guy I need. The kind of guy who'd be *right* for me.

Such a bummer I don't want what's right! Not at this juncture, in any case.

I spot my *wrong* kind of guy and his wrong kind of pet from afar. They're engrossed in a game of catch. Noah hurls a stick. His four-legged friend races after it and brings it back. But instead of giving it to his master, he keeps it between his clenched jaws, bounces around Noah, and wags his tail.

Noah picks up another stick and throws it. Oscar drops the one in his mouth and zooms to snatch the second stick. When he returns with it, Noah pets him and hurls the first stick.

"Doing what you do would drive me mad," I say after Noah and I exchange greetings.

"It's not so bad," Noah says. "Oscar loves this game."

I point at the stick in Oscar's mouth. "Isn't he supposed to give that to you?"

"I'm sure he's considered it." Noah shrugs. "But he prefers to keep it for himself."

"How very… un-doglike."

"I told you he's part cat."

I smirk. "Yeah, you did."

"It's not just the failure to fetch, there are other symptoms." He crouches and begins to play tug-of-war with his dog. "Oscar takes five or six catnaps during the day, with the first one beginning a few minutes after he wakes up in the morning."

"Why does he even bother waking up?"

"So he can relocate to my bed."

"Right."

"But I can close the bedroom door for the night," he adds quickly. "Oscar will take his first morning nap in his own bed."

I finger my watch strap. "Can you make him purr?"

Noah nods. "Oscar, sit!"

Oscar looks at him, then at me and then at Noah again. After Noah repeats the command three more times, Oscar sighs and sits down. Noah squats next to him and rubs Oscar's throat. The dog makes a soft guttural sound you wouldn't expect from a canine, Noah scratches him behind his ears, and Oscar purrs louder.

"Satisfied?" Noah asks me.

"Awed," I say.

When we get to his apartment, Oscar rushes to his water bowl and drinks thirstily.

Noah kicks off his flip-flops. "You can keep yours on, if you want."

"No problem." I slip out of my clogs. "The floor looks clean enough."

"It *is* clean," he says, heading to the kitchen.

I follow him.

Noah opens the *rosé* and pours me a glass. "At what time do you usually eat dinner?"

"Nine-ish. Typically a salad or a bowl of soup."

"I made a Caesar salad with chicken breast and mixed greens," he declares not without pride and glances at the clock on the wall. "Will you be hungry enough in an hour?"

"Think so."

A loud snore comes from the TV room, and I give Noah a quizzical look.

"Oscar's last nap before bedtime," he explains.

"Is he... *snoring?*"

"Uh-huh."

"Cats don't snore." I quirk an eyebrow. "Neither do dogs, to my knowledge."

"He's also part human," Noah says, bounding around the table to plant himself next to me.

"Of course he is."

Noah's gaze settles on my lips and my heart begins to pound.

I point to the *rosé*. "I thought you were a beer buff."

"Nah. I'm a wine person. I only drink beer in July and August to prevent my body from overheating."

"A wine lover, huh?" I tilt my head to the side, eyeing him up and down.

He smirks. "I don't fit the image of a wine connoisseur, do I?"

I smile apologetically.

He shrugs. "Appearances can be deceptive."

"So can words." I jut out my chin in defiance. "What can you tell me about this wine, for instance, since you're a *connoisseur*?"

Picking up the bottle, he says, "Côtes de Provence Saint Victoire, 2015 vintage. A great Provence *rosé*. Dry with a hint of berries. It's excellent with chicken, so be sure to leave some for the meal."

I lift my glass to my nose and sniff. "Anything else?"

"This wine comes from the vineyards of the Négrel family in Provence," Noah says. "They've been making it for 200 years."

My eyebrows crawl up. Could he be bluffing, inventing all this stuff on the fly? Unlikely. But even if he is, he deserves kudos for creativity.

"Cheers," I say.

"Cheers." He touches his glass to mine.

We stare into each other's eyes as we drink.

Noah's blue gaze holds such unambiguous intent, I cannot but respond. His desire is contagious. This man has accomplished quite a feat, come to think of it. He turns me on. I know I'll enjoy his touch and I'm almost certain I'll like his kisses.

It's what he'll do afterward that has me on edge.

The doorbell rings.

Oscar runs to the foyer. When Noah and I get there, the dog is sitting in front of the door, wagging his tail. He looks at Noah with an almost palpable joy in his black eyes, like he knows who's on the other side and is happy to see them.

Noah opens the door to a coquettish gray-haired woman.

Oscar begins to dance around her until she pets him and lets him give her a few generous licks. Then she straightens up and notices me.

"Oh my!" She turns to Noah. "I'm so sorry. I didn't know you had company tonight."

"That's all right, Juliet," Noah says. "Meet my friend Sophie."

Juliet grabs me by the shoulders and cheek kisses me. "So pleased to meet you, darling."

"The pleasure is mine," I say, unsure how to act around this exuberant woman or what to think of her.

"Hamlet and I just realized we've left our phone charger in the summer house," she says to Noah. "I was wondering if we could borrow yours until I go to Darty tomorrow and buy a new one."

"Sure thing," Noah says, heading down the hallway.

To the bedroom, I presume. Which I'll most likely discover later tonight. I exhale a shallow breath.

"Hamlet—that's my husband—is too dependent on his phone," Juliet explains to me. "Email, Facebook, Solitaire… Me? I only ever remember I have a phone when someone calls me. Are you a smartphone addict, too?"

"I'm somewhere between you and your husband," I say with a smile.

She smiles back. "You're even prettier than Noah said."

"He told you about me?"

"Just that he's been hanging out with a lovely American girl."

"I see."

Noah returns with a charger and hands it to Juliet.

"Guess what," she says to him. "I'm making your favorite *boreks*, tabbouleh, and dolma next Sunday."

Noah widens his eyes. "All three at once?"

She nods smugly. "Why don't the both of you come over for dinner?"

"You *must* taste Juliet's dolma," Noah says to me before I can invent a polite excuse. "It's out of this world. And her *boreks* are to die for."

"What's a borek?" I ask.

Juliet gives me a sympathetic look, sighs, and shakes her head as if to say she's really sorry about my sad *borek*-less life. But she doesn't offer a definition.

Neither does Noah.

"I have a prior—" I begin.

"That's settled, then." Juliet pats my cheek. "See you at dinnertime next Sunday, darling."

She waves good-bye to Noah and crosses the landing to her apartment.

I wait until Noah has shut the door behind her and cross my arms over my chest. "Did I just get signed up for a dinner with total strangers even though I was saying no thanks?"

He gives me a please-don't-shoot-me look. "You don't have to go if you really hate the sound of it, but trust me, you'll miss out on the best dolma this side of the Seine."

I sigh and unfold my arms. "Fine, fine."

"Cool," he says, grinning.

"I assume I just met *Madame* Derzian, right?"

"Correct."

"And her first name is Juliet."

He nods.

I narrow my eyes. "And her husband's name is Hamlet."

He nods again.

"They are *well matched*." I bite my bottom lip to stifle a smile.

"Don't laugh," Noah says.

"Sorry."

"I mean, don't laugh *yet*, not until you hear what they've named their children."

"Tell me."

"Their son's name is Romeo, and their daughter is called Ophelia."

This is too precious to be true. "You're messing with me."

"I swear I'm not," he says, drawing closer. "It's their Armenian sense of humor. Ever heard of Radio Yerevan?"

I shake my head.

"They're famous for their political jokes," he says. "My father was a big fan."

Is there a touch of nostalgia in Noah's voice at the mention of his "nasty piece of work" dad? Something doesn't compute…

"An example?" I ask.

He wrinkles his brow. "I can think of only one right now, and it isn't political."

"That's OK."

"Radio Yerevan was asked, *What's an exchange of opinions?*" Noah pauses for effect. "Radio Yerevan answered, *It's when you enter your boss's office with your opinion and walk out with his.*"

I giggle, following him back to the kitchen.

Noah sets his glass on the table. "Back to the Derzians. Obviously, Juliet and Hamlet didn't fall in love to form a Shakespearean couple. It was a coincidence."

"That's good to know," I say, wondering what his next move will be.

"Both names just happened to be popular among Lebanese Armenians at the time." He takes my glass from my hand and places it next to his. "But their children's names are quite intentional."

"Why?" I ask.

"It was Juliet's idea. Apparently, Hamlet wasn't too keen, but she couldn't resist the temptation."

I shake my head in fake reproof. "Women."

"Hear, hear!" He encases my face with his big hands and stares at my mouth as if he wants to devour it.

I suppose, that's exactly what he wants given the hunger in his darkened eyes.

"I sometimes wonder," he says, his gaze still on my lips, "if women enjoy watching a man almost lose it with want."

His voice is hoarse and incredibly sexy.

Those hands on my cheeks, that voice, that look…

"Wonder no more," I murmur. "They do."

Without any warning, his mouth is on mine. He presses a soft kiss to my lips and my eyelids drop. Stroking my face, he brushes his lips over my chin, jawline, and throat, before returning to my mouth.

I kiss him back. His lips are warm and a little wet from the wine.

While both of his hands still cup my face, Noah sweeps his tongue over my lower lip. He lingers in the right corner of my mouth, kisses it, and moves to the left corner.

I force my eyelids to open so I can watch his face while he's kissing me like this. What I see is sexy as hell. His eyes are glazed over with desire, his ruggedly handsome face flushed with need.

I don't know about women in general, but admittedly frigid Sophie Bander enjoys watching a man almost lose it with want.

If that man is Noah Masson.

"Sophie," he rasps against my mouth.

A shiver runs down my spine.

He slides the tip of his tongue between my lips, coaxing me to open them.

I do, gladly.

Next thing I know, we're both lost in a hot, raw, openmouthed kiss. I feel lightheaded as his tongue thrusts against my palate and strokes the inside of my teeth. When he caresses my tongue, I stroke his, getting drunk on his delicious wine-infused taste. I hear myself moan softly.

I could cry with how sweet this moment is.

Why didn't anyone tell me kissing could feel like this?

Even with our mouths joined, there's still a good inch between our bodies. Noah slides one hand down the side of my neck. For a few moments, he rests it— hot and fingers splayed—at the back of my shoulders. Then, applying the tiniest amount of pressure, he nudges me closer until my nipples touch his chest.

Through two thin layers of fabric, the contact sets off a spark, electrifying me. My nipples are engorged and rock hard. I had no idea they could be like this.

Noah's kiss grows hungrier, rougher. Gripping the back of my head, he draws me as close as possible without crushing me against his chest.

I delve my hand into his soft wavy hair as I revel in being held like this, kissed like this, desired like this by a man I haven't been able to stop thinking about since meeting him.

When he breaks away, I follow his lips, hungry for more.

"Sophie," he says, taking a step back. "Wait. There's something I need to ask first."

With an enormous effort, I steady myself and focus on his eyes.

He takes a deep breath. "Are you sure it's me you want?"

THIRTEEN
Noah

She blinks. "What?"

"I wouldn't want to…"—I search for a good word—"derail you."

She stares at me, still confused.

Cut to the chase, Noah. Ask her the question you know you should've asked already, before you brought her here, before you pulled her into your arms in the bivvy.

Even if it means shooting yourself in the foot.

I tip my head back for a second and look straight into her beautiful eyes. "What about Zach?"

"Ah," she breathes out as comprehension hits her.

"Isn't it *him* you really want?"

"I do," she says. "I mean, not *your* Zach, but someone like him in a couple of years when I'm back in Key West and ready to settle down."

I exhale slowly.

She smiles. "But right now, here on my Parisian internship-slash-holiday, it's *you* that I want."

My shoulders sag with relief.

Keeping Sophie for me when I'm supposed to set her up with Zach still doesn't feel kosher. But, at least, I know where I stand now. Sophie isn't kissing me because she can't decide between me and Zach or because Zach is taking too long to ask her out.

She's kissing me because she chose me.

Even if it's just for the duration of her Parisian holiday. Actually, that's fine by me. More than fine— it's perfect. Haven't I, too, been thinking of another woman for when I'm ready to settle down?

I peer at Sophie, taking in the bounty the universe deemed appropriate to drop onto my lap.

She chuckles softly. "You look like you just won Olympic gold."

"It feels that way," I admit.

Taking a step toward her, I back her against the wall, lean in, and place my hands on either side of her face.

Her smile slips, giving way to a wild mixture of emotions that flicker in her expressive eyes. There's desire and excitement, for sure, but there's also anxiety. Not surprising, given her history of ham-handed men.

I'll tread softly.

"Bébé," I say planting a gentle kiss to her forehead. "If I start doing something you don't like, or don't feel ready for, just say it. OK?"

She nods, her expression relaxing. "Go easy, please?"

"I promise."

She places her hands on my chest, stroking it. Her lovely fingers trail my collarbones, my throat, run down my shoulders, and then return to my chest.

"You're perfect," she says. "Better than my secret fantasy."

"What's your fantasy?"

She cocks her head. "Don't you know the meaning of the word *secret*?"

"Have mercy!" I plead. "Now that you disclosed you have a secret fantasy, you *must* tell me what it is, or I'll wither and die of frustration."

She hesitates for a brief moment and shrugs. "Oh well, here goes. My secret fantasy has always been a blue-eyed American football quarterback."

A happy grin spreads on my face, no matter how hard I try to suppress it.

Her gaze zeroes in on my pectorals. "But I'll take a French water polo goalie any day."

"Take him today," I say, catching her chin between my thumb and forefinger.

And then I kiss her hard, the way I've been dying to kiss her for several weeks now.

She lets me. Better than that, she responds, delving her hands into my hair. Her heavenly breath—chocolate, wine, and Sophie—makes me wild with lust. As I explore the tender interior of her mouth, a sense of urgency comes over me. I haven't forgotten my promise to go easy, and I'm fully prepared to freeze the moment she lets me know it's too much, or too soon. But until that moment, I'll push my sweet Sophie to see how far she'll let me go.

I break the kiss.

She sways, panting, her eyes glazed with desire.

"Bedroom." I say. "Unless you want me to take you right here up against this wall."

Say yes.

The image of Sophie impaled on my cock, back to the wall, makes my hands tremble. I picture her in that position—legs locked around my waist, breasts bared and bobbing as I pound into her with all I've got.

Jesus Christ.

What happened to not rushing it? So much for my self-control... The need in my loins is killing all my good intentions. This woman has bewitched me.

The moment those words form in my mind, shame hits me in the solar plexus, making me choke.

What's wrong with you, man?

Blaming a woman's charms for your own failure to show restraint is... cheap, to put it mildly. It's what bad lovers do. It's what rapists do.

Say no, Sophie.

She blinks and swallows. "Bedroom."

Thank you!

I grab her hand and lead her through the TV room to the bedroom.

It's bathed in the golden light of the setting sun as we enter.

I turn to Sophie. "Too much light?"

She nods.

I go to the window and draw the curtains, leaving a narrow gap. When I return by her side, she's already taken her shorts off and is reaching for the hem of her tee. I watch, mesmerized. She pulls it up over her tummy, breasts, and over her head.

Spellbound, I follow her every move.

Sophie lowers her arms and drops her T-shirt to the floor.

I suck in a sharp breath, awed by what she's uncovered to my eyes.

Wrapped in a flimsy cotton bra with a floral pattern and a tiny pink bow tie in the middle, her pert, full breasts are the best gift I've ever received. They're perfection itself—the very essence of femininity. Her erect nipples pebble the fabric in the center of each breast.

I kind of knew already her breasts were out of this world—summer materials don't leave much to the imagination—but seeing them like this robs my lungs of air.

I yank off my T and take a step toward her.

She reaches for my belt and tugs on it. My breaths come shallow and fast, as she undoes the buckle and draws the zipper of my jeans down. Slowly, she works my pants down my hips and thighs. When they fall to the floor, I step out of them.

She stares at my tented boxer briefs.

If only I could tell if it's anticipation or anxiety that heaves her chest!

She unclasps her bra, freeing her gorgeous boobs. I cup the left one, and nearly growl with the pleasure of it. Her breast is firm, soft and smooth, and it fits snugly in my palm as if it belongs there. Which it does.

I cover her right breast with my other hand, and just hold her like that for a moment.

She smiles. "Big hands and a good grip are definitely an asset, huh?"

"I'm glad you agree," I mutter as I begin to fondle the treasure in my hands and kiss every inch of her face.

A good ten minutes later, I slip my thumbs into the waistband of her panties and push them over her hips and down her thighs.

My hand slides between her legs before she's done shaking her panties off her ankle. I can't wait. Backing her to the bed, I yank off my briefs, crawl up, and loom over her.

Beneath me is a woman hotter and more beautiful than anything I've ever seen.

Regardless of what she believes, she was made for sex *with me.*

Pressing the ball of my palm against her mound, I rub and slip a finger inside. She's wet. Not soaked, but definitely wet. I pull my finger out and position myself at her entrance.

"I don't have protection," she says.

"Not to worry, I got a whole pa—" I begin, my gaze trained on the thatch between her legs, before I realize she's hyperventilating.

I look up.

She swallows hard, clearly panicked, her eyes darting to the door.

Fuck.

"Bummer," I say. "I don't have any, either."

The relief in her eyes makes my chest clench.

I roll off her and lie on my side. "That second guy you told me about… Did he rape you?"

"No," she says. "Maybe. I don't know. I *did* agree to have sex with him. I told myself it was bound to be better than the first time. But once we were naked, and he started groping me and kissing me… suddenly, I didn't want it anymore."

She searches my face as if her default assumption is that I won't understand.

"Did you tell him you wanted to call it off?" I ask.

"Yes, but he wouldn't listen. He explained later that he'd been too far gone by then. I couldn't seriously expect him to be able to stop at that point."

"Did you believe him?"

"I guess." She furrows her brow. "I don't know how men function."

"Psychopaths aside, we function like humans," I say. "Not savage beasts. If we *want* to stop when a woman says no, we *can* stop."

I turn away and reach for my underwear on the floor.

She tugs at my arm. "Wait. I'm not saying no to… everything."

I tilt my head to the side. "You'll have to be more specific."

She looks away, blushing.

If I were a true gentleman, noble in my heart and not just on paper, I'd let her off the hook at this point. I'd make suggestions and ask her to respond with a yes or no. But I'm too keen on hearing her talk dirty.

"Come on, Sophie," I encourage her. "You can do it."

She grimaces. "Do I really have to spell it out?"

"I'm afraid you do."

"Oral sex," she mutters under her breath.

I cup my ear. "Beg your pardon? Did you say something?"

She chews on her lower lip, looking utterly miserable.

I can't believe how much fun it is to tease her.

"Oral sex," she repeats louder. "I'd like some oral sex, please. If that's OK with you."

I struggle to keep a straight face. "Would you like to give me a blowjob or do you prefer that I go down on you?"

"You," she whispers.

I push her legs apart and sit between them.

Suddenly, I don't feel like joking anymore.

I bend down and nuzzle the insides of her thighs. Then I kiss her folds openmouthed, spreading her with my fingers. I give her a hard, long lick and dip my tongue in. She tastes like sex in its purest form. Sweet, spicy, addictive.

I probe her, pushing a little deeper with each thrust of my tongue. She begins to whimper. That's all the encouragement I need to involve a finger, so I can lick her at the same time. Sophie's whimpers turn into moans, and soon she's writhing on the bed and gripping my hair.

My cock aches.

The temptation to shift so I can grind it against her, or—even better—so she could caress it is so strong I almost give in. But, in the end, I don't budge. Tonight isn't about me—it's about Sophie.

Only her.

When I glance up at her face, Sophie's eyes are closed, her mouth slightly open, and her cheeks flushed. So hot. Feeling her arousal bathe my finger in warm waves, I go harder, greedier, sucking and nipping at her flesh.

She tenses and spasms around me.

With a growl coming from a deep, previously unknown place in my chest, I lick her orgasm clean.

Then I stretch out by her side and gather her to me.

She gives me a heavy-lidded look, lifts her head, and takes my mouth in a smoldering kiss.

When she breaks it, I stare at her face. "Did you like your taste?"

"I did." She grins. "Is that weird?"

"Not in my view, *bébé*." I run my thumb over her lips. "Then again, my view is remote and unfocused right now."

She gives me a quizzical look.

I open my arms and spread them like a bird's wings. "Cause I'm flying."

FOURTEEN
Sophie

I wake up to Oscar licking my face.

"Yikes, get off me, beast!" I shoo him away from my head, wiping my mouth, chin, and cheeks with the sheet.

Noah levers his body into a sitting position and nudges Oscar toward the edge of the bed. "Bad boy."

Honestly, he could've put a little more heart into his admonishment. At least for show.

When the dog jumps to the floor, Noah turns to me, smiling. "Congratulations."

"For what?"

"On Oscar's upgrading you from harmless to lick-worthy."

"Does he upgrade everyone so fast or should I feel proud and special?" I ask archly.

"Definitely proud and special." He gives me a wink. "And not because of Oscar."

"No?"

"He got nothing on *me*."

"How so?"

His smile broadens. "When I first saw you, it took me less than ten seconds to upgrade you from harmless to lick-worthy."

Memories of last night flood my brain, and I turn away, hoping he won't notice my flaming ears. "Can I go to the shower first?"

"Of course."

I roll out of the bed, kneel, and sift through the pile of clothes on the floor, looking for my underwear. I find my bra, but not my panties.

"Oops," Noah says, leaning over the other side of the bed and prying my lacy boy shorts from Oscar's mouth.

The garment is wet as he holds it up for me.

Seeing my hesitation, he balls it into his fist. "I'm—we—are very sorry about this. I'll wash it."

"I can't go home commando."

"May I offer you a pair of my briefs or Speedos?" he asks with a smile dancing in the corner of his mouth.

I jerk my chin up. "This is *not* funny."A

"You're right," he says. "I'll have a word with Oscar."

He jumps out of the bed, hunkers next to his dog and schools his features into a stern expression. "That was badly done, Oscar. Very bad."

Oscar listens carefully, his big sad eyes locked on Noah.

"In this house, we don't munch on our guests' underwear without permission," Noah continues, his tone falsely stern. "You should be ashamed of—"

Oscar rears up and gives Noah's nose a happy lick.

Noah shuts up mid sentence, a grin breaking across his face.

I shake my head. "If that's how you discipline him, I see why he does as he pleases."

"Have you ever tried scolding someone while they're licking your nose?"

"No, I haven't."

He pets Oscar. "Thought so. F.Y.I, it's impossible."

"If you say so." I let out a resigned sigh. "Hey, I'll take you up on your offer of underwear."

He opens one of the drawers in the closet and rummages through its contents.

"This should do the trick," he says, handing me a pair of stretchy boxer briefs.

I grab them and head to the bathroom.

Twenty minutes later, I enter the kitchen. It smells of freshly brewed coffee and warm pastries.

I point at the croissants on the table. "Microwave?"

He screws his face up in exaggerated affront. "Please. I bought them in the *boulangerie* downstairs while you were in the shower."

"Now I know why my friend Sue suggested I spend a night with a Frenchman," I say before biting into a delicious roll.

"And why's that?"

"This *perfection*"—I hold the croissant up—"with fresh coffee early in the morning. So worth all the hassle."

His lips quirk as he points to the bottle of *rosé* from last night. "I'd say *this* was worth the hassle.

I cock my head. "You're well informed about wines for an athlete who grew up in Nepal."

"The French are born well informed about wines," he says. "Ask your mother, if you don't believe me."

"I may not know much about wines," I say, "But I do know a thing or two about vineyards."

"How come?"

"We had a two-day workshop at the agency last week on vineyard property sales. I learned an awful lot."

"Like what?"

"Like, whether the estate has a winery or only a vineyard, the type of grapes it grows, the age of the vines, their yield, if there's staff already on payroll, and lots of other things. All of them affect the price of the estate."

"I had no idea," he says, looking impressed. "Would love to hear more."

I smile, flattered. "Sure, but bear in mind I just had a crash course. There are specialized brokers out there who can immediately say if the estate is going to be profitable."

"I think your knowledge will suffice for my purposes," he says enigmatically.

Before I can ask him what he means, my phone wakes up in my purse, emitting Dad's ringtone.

I answer it.

"Hey, Princess, I have great news," Dad says. "Last night, Doug Thompson insisted we go out for a drink—"

"Our archenemy Doug Thompson?"

"Not anymore. He confessed he's in love with you, can you believe it?"

"No," I say.

"He's been in love with you for years now," Dad plows on, "and he'll do anything for a chance to win your heart."

I'm too flabbergasted to respond.

"If you and Doug hit it off, we could merge our two agencies and become an undisputed market leader. We'd have no rival in the Keys. We could develop the Parisian thing you started into a real agency, and—why not—open one in Miami."

He's so excited I can hardly believe my ears. "Dad, I—"

"You don't have to say or do anything about it right now," he cuts in. "I just wanted you to begin seeing Doug in a different light. If he's no longer our competitor, he's exactly what you want in a man."

This conversation is getting way too sensitive.

"Can I call you back in ten minutes?" I ask.

There's a brief pause before he says, "You're not alone."

"That's right."

"At eight in the morning," he adds pointedly.

His voice is icy now compared to the warmth it bubbled with seconds ago.

"I'll call you back," I say and hang up.

Noah hands me a fragrant cup of coffee. "Drink this before you run away."

I gulp down the contents and give him a smooch.

As soon I'm on the street, I dial Dad.

"You've met someone," he says.

"Maybe."

"Is he black?"

When did race become a factor?

"No," I say. "Neither is Doug Thompson, last time I checked."

"It's different."

"How?"

"Doug is a local, a native conch born and raised in Key West."

"Is that a virtue?" I ask with a touch of sarcasm.

"Yes, it is," Dad says. "It means he has roots here. It means he can put up with our summers, and he won't run away after a few years to a cooler climate."

Sheesh.

This is about Mom as much as it's about Doug. I should've seen it coming.

"I take it he's French," Dad says.

"Yes."

"Catholic."

"He isn't religious."

"Even worse—an atheist."

"I don't think he's an atheist—he just doesn't give religion much thought. His passion is something else."

"What?"

"Water polo."

"Hmm. Is he a pro? Is he making good money?"

"Water polo isn't like baseball or soccer. It doesn't pay very well. That's why he has a part-time job."

"Doing what?"

I hesitate. Dad isn't going to like this. *Oh, well.* "He delivers pizzas."

Silence.

"Dad?"

"You're dating a pizza delivery man."

I don't comment.

He clears his throat. "Does your delivery man have a college degree?"

"Um… I don't know."

"So, basically, he's a loser," Dad says before adding, "Euro-trash."

"Oh, come on!"

"He'll pull you down, Sophie, can't you see that?"

"Dad, I don't plan on marrying him." I pout in frustration. "Shouldn't you be happy I'm finally dating someone?"

"You're dating someone who lives in Europe and delivers pizzas. No, I'm not happy."

"He's a wonderful person," I say, "and a gifted goalkeeper."

I wish I could mention Noah's additional gift that I discovered last night, but this is Dad, not Mom.

"A pizza guy." He laughs bitterly. "Ain't he a catch?"

I say nothing.

"What's his name?" Dad asks.

"Noah Masson."

"Just keep your head on your shoulders, Princess, will you?" Dad's tone is placating now. "You're young and inexperienced, and this Noah person… Can you promise me you won't do anything rash?"

"No problem," I say and we hang up.

Big problem, actually.

Despite Dad's outright disapproval and my own misgivings, I may have crossed the red line already.

I may be falling for Noah.

FIFTEEN
Noah

I stare at Diane's latest missive while my mind processes what I've just read.

Dear Noah,

Jaqueline tells me you visited the chateau last week. That's such good news! I shared it with Sebastian who didn't comment, but his eyes lit up with renewed hope. Did the place bring back any childhood memories? Did it call to you? I want to believe it did.

<u>*Sidenote:*</u> *I'm not usually this sentimental. It's the baby blues. It'll pass (fingers crossed).*

Anyway, back to the reason I'm writing. Thinking about your visit to the estate made me realize something. Since you've been refusing to meet with Seb, or even Raphael, you may have never had a chance to hear Sebastian's side of the story.

I'm going to give it to you in this letter, and you can do what you want with it.

Marguerite ran out of money and asked Sebastian to donate half a million to her charity shortly after your father passed. I believe you know that much. What you may not know is that the company was on the brink of ruin at that point.

Sebastian said no to her because he was investing his personal inheritance—every last cent of it— into Parfums d'Arcy. If he'd sent her the amount she was asking for, there was no chance he could save the company. Almost a thousand workers in France and abroad would have lost their jobs.

I'm not saying it was the only factor in Sebastian's decision, but it was a major one.

What would you do in his place? Would you forego the last chance to save the family business so you could help people in a foreign country? Maybe you would. But Sebastian chose differently. And his choice doesn't make him a bad person.

Seb asked Marguerite if she could put her foundation on hold and volunteer for other nonprofits while he's saving the business. She wouldn't hear of it.

Two years later, Parfums d'Arcy turned a modest profit. Your brother offered it to Marguerite, even though he was hoping to reinvest it into the company. She told him she'd found another solution, and no longer needed the d'Arcy money or his help.

So, there you have it—Sebastian's side of the story.

On another note, we are all hoping to see you at Raphael and Mia's wedding. Please come. It would be the best wedding present Raphael could dream of. Trust me.

Diane

I'm not going. When you cut someone off, there's no point in doing it *partially*.

Do I believe her version of Sebastian's side of the story? Could it be true? Is it possible that my brothers aren't moved by greed alone? Was Sebastian really concerned about the fate of his workers? Did he really offer his first profit to Maman?

Have I been judging him too harshly?

As for Raphael, Maman always says he was too young at the time and too easily influenced.

Speaking of Maman, something in Diane's letter bothers me more than the possibility I've been wrong to cut my brothers off. It's the response Maman gave Seb when he finally offered some money.

She told him she'd found another solution.

This "other solution" could only be Pierre Sorrel, the foreign ministry official who helped Maman get French government funding that year, and the years that followed. The ultimate jerk who made her pay for his help with her body.

That's what she told me the day I came home from school earlier than usual and saw him in our living room. He had his back to the door, ass naked, pants around his ankles. Maman was on her knees in front of him...

My hands ball into fists as I remember the scene.

What wouldn't I give to unsee it! I was fourteen and Maman was my hero, a warrior for social justice, a saint. When Sorrel ran out, and she confessed that what I'd seen was the price she was paying to continue her work, I resolved to kill him. I spent countless sleepless nights plotting his murder to save Maman from his clutches.

But the one time I actually had a chance at fifteen during a garden party at the French Embassy, I couldn't do it.

That's why I'm so mad at my brothers.

That is why I can't forgive them.

But... why didn't Maman take Sebastian's money when he offered it so she could be free of Sorrel? Was her pride stronger than her misery? Or was she less miserable than she led me to believe?

I shake my head.

This is all conjecture based on secondhand information from a woman who's far from impartial. Diane loves Seb, and she goes out of her way to justify his actions. Quite successfully, in fact. Every time she writes, I end up questioning things I've always known to be true.

I crumple her letter and toss it in the trash can. The next one she sends me will end up there unopened.

Anger pulsing in my veins, I grab my backpack and head out. Sophie and I have a train to catch.

We're traveling to Burgundy.

It's my second trip there in the space of a week. I went to the Chateau d'Arcy last Saturday to talk with the housekeeper, Jacqueline Bruel. Since my twenty-seventh birthday two weeks ago, I'm the legal owner of the estate, which means *Madame* Bruel is in my employ.

Not for long, though.

When Jacqueline and I chatted last week, I asked her to make sure the staff clear the premises from two to six this afternoon so I could spend a few hours there on my own and decide what I want to do with it.

I lied. My decision is made. It was made years ago. I'm taking Sophie to the estate today so she can give me an initial assessment and a ballpark price. Then I'll entrust it to one of those specialized brokers she mentioned.

And then I'll sell it.

* * *

When Sophie and I climb out of the cab and walk past the wrought iron gates, the air smells of roses and grass. Bumblebees and other summer bugs buzz over the neatly trimmed hedgerow.

A soft breeze makes thousands of oak leaves rustle along the gravel driveway. An English-style park of vast lawns sprinkled with sprawling trees and colorful flowerbeds begins to our left and stretches behind the castle. A vineyard spreads outward from it, covering the soft slopes of the hills to our right.

All of this is such a contrast to the smells, views, and sounds of Paris that it's hard to believe we left the city less than three hours ago.

Oscar would love it here.

He'd chase butterflies and roll on the grass to his heart's content, and there'd be no one to kick him out because it's a no-poop zone.

"Your friend Sebastian is smart to sell his chateau in the summer." Sophie fills her lungs with air and looks around. "I've been here less than a minute and already I'm in love."

I give her a stiff smile, wondering if I'd named my imaginary friend "Sebastian" by coincidence.

Hardly. I guess it was an unconscious attempt to give this charade a touch of truth.

Sebastian, Raphael and I, and generations of d'Arcy boys and girls before us, spent many happy summers here. Raph and I always got in trouble, climbing trees we were too chicken to descend, chasing the housekeeper's pet goose around the park and playing hide-and-seek where we weren't allowed to.

What a shame my easygoing middle brother sided with Seb when Maman needed him!

Unlike his younger siblings, the always serious Sebastian spent most of his waking hours in the library, reading clever books. I'm sure it's in the library that he first hatched his plan for world domination.

"Again, why is your buddy selling this?" Sophie asks.

"He needs money."

"And he's stuck abroad, right?"

"Right." I turn away. "Where would you like to begin?"

"What are my options?"

"The park, the vineyard, or the house."

She points her chin to the stairs leading up to the ornate entrance. "Let's see the castle first."

"Sure," I nod before clapping my hand to my forehead. "Almost forgot. We won't have time to check it out, but you should know there's a grotto with rock art just a short hike up that hill."

I point in the direction of the d'Arcy Grotto.

"Is it part of the estate?" she asks.

I nod.

"Is the grotto any good?"

"It has the oldest prehistoric rock paintings in France," I say, a proud note creeping into my voice. "Ice Age about forty thousand years ago. I remember the magnificent mammoths and reindeer. Lions, too."

"Did you stay here as a kid?"

"Yeah."

"How sad," she says.

"That I visited the estate as a child?"

"No, silly. That your friend is selling his childhood home."

"It isn't sad," I say. "He doesn't care for this place."

Really, he doesn't.

SIXTEEN
Sophie

"How old is this chateau?" I ask when we've reached the top of the stairs.

Noah unlocks the beautifully carved entrance door. "More than four hundred years."

"Is it listed as a historical monument?"

He nods.

"It means the new owners won't be able to make any big changes without a special permit," I say.

Noah gives me a worried look. "Why would they want to make big changes?"

"Does the chateau have an indoor swimming pool and a spa?"

He shakes his head.

"Non-European buyers would likely want those things."

"Right."

I look around, taking in the vast foyer flooded with soft light, the marble flooring, the imposing chandeliers and fixtures, and the majestic staircase that leads to the second floor.

"This way." Noah motions to a drawing room on the other side of the foyer.

The chipped marble under our feet changes to an intricately set art parquet. The floor creaks with every step we take, but it's beautiful. Small honey-colored panels—probably oak—come together in large diagonal squares. I've seen this design before. I close my eyes, recalling what Véronique taught me about traditional French flooring styles.

"Parquet de Versailles," I announce with pride, pointing down. "That's what this pattern is called."

Noah smiles. "Good to know."

"Don't you go all smug on me, goalie." I jerk my chin up. "You brought me here so you could hear my opinions on this property, did you not?"

He drops his head to his chest. "*Désolé.* I did."

"I tried to look up this estate last night, but I couldn't find a chateau called Thouars-Maurice."

"No?" He stares out the window.

"Are you sure you got the name right?"

"I'll check with my buddy," he says. "Maybe the official name is slightly different."

"I bet it is."

Peeling my gaze off Noah, I look around. "This room is… unbelievable."

He grins. "It's called Salon Bleu."

I can see why. The walls are covered in faded blue murals depicting pretty shepherd girls frolicking with naughty shepherd boys in bucolic settings. I doubt Noah will be able to give me the age of these murals, but they must be at least a couple hundred years old.

The only mural-free wall has tall French doors that open to an English-style park, some of which we saw from the front of the building.

The view takes my breath away.

Surveying generous lawns that meld into meadows to meet woodlands in the distance, I declare that this is the most beautiful sight I've ever seen.

Even the ocean sunsets back home can't compare

"This view is gold," I say to Noah. "Make sure nothing obstructs it when buyers come."

"Your word is my command."

"If I were you—or your friend—I'd put a big comfy armchair right here." I point to the space between the fireplace and the French doors. "And an open book on top."

"Wouldn't it look messy?"

"It will look lived-in and help the prospective buyers imagine themselves in this salon."

"Very clever."

"Just a little realtor trick."

"Got any others up your sleeve?"

I give him a cocky *what-do-you-think* look.

He grins and pulls me to him. "I love it when you act naughty."

"This is nothing, babes," I purr, emboldened by his compliment. "You haven't seen me naughty yet."

Nobody has seen me naughty yet, to be exact, but there's no need to mention that.

Noah's hand makes its way down my back and lingers on my backside. "Let me show you the great hall before we make it to the bedrooms."

I raise my eyebrows.

He couldn't possibly be suggesting what I think he's suggesting.

Or could he?

He takes my hand and leads me to another salon, bigger and grander than the one we just admired. There's a small pedestal table planted in the middle of the ballroom. A bottle of red wine, a corkscrew and two stemmed glasses form an inviting group on top of it.

Noah picks up the bottle whose label reads, *Coteau de la lune*. While he's studying it, I spot a note, written in a neat schoolteacher's hand.

> *We hope you enjoy this twenty-year-old Pinot Noir—the chateau's last vintage.*
>
> *Jacqueline, Greg, Deolinda, and Fabrice*

I show the note to Noah. "Who are these people?"

"The staff."

"Are they invisible?"

He smirks. "They've taken the afternoon off so we can snoop around undisturbed."

How unusual.

Noah opens the bottle and pours a little wine into one of the glasses. He sniffs it, takes a sip, and fills both glasses.

"*A la tienne,*" he says, touching his glass to mine.

I take a small sip. The wine is full-bodied and rich in subtle flavors I wish I could identify. One thing I'm sure of—the chateau had a damn good vintage twenty years back.

"Do you know why they stopped making wine?"

"Sebastian's father died," Noah says. "He'd been the *vigneron* of the family."

He sets his glass on the table. "Come on, let's go. We have a dozen bedrooms to check out, not to mention the park and the vineyard."

As I follow him up the gorgeous but rickety staircase and down a long hallway, I notice how dilapidated the castle is behind its regal grandeur and refinement. It's squeaky clean, but no amount of dusting and polishing can hide the mildew stains on crumbling walls or the huge cracks in the ceiling.

"When was this castle last refurbished?" I ask Noah.

"In the sixties."

He knows quite a bit about this place. Of course, his friend Sebastian probably gave him all the important details.

Noah opens one of the doors and motions me into a spacious room. "This is the lord and lady's chamber."

"The floors will need to be refinished here," I say. "And the walls treated and replastered."

After that we check out a magnificent wood-paneled library and five or six smaller bedrooms with en suite bathrooms. Some of them have paintwork or fabrics on the walls, others boast ceiling beams and antique bathtubs. All are as delightful as they are run-down.

In one of the rooms, he backs me to the wall and kisses me until I'm weak in the knees.

"Tomorrow?" he asks, staring into my eyes.

I know what he means without needing to ask. "Tomorrow."

He flashes me a big, sexy grin.

I grin back, excited and scared in equal measure.

"Want to look at the vines now?" he asks, drawing back. "Or continue exploring the remaining guest rooms, drawing rooms, wine cellars and the kitchens?"

I glance at my watch. "Our train leaves in less than two hours. So, yeah, let's see the vineyard."

We exit the castle and head toward the hillside, passing a small chapel, a fountain and an incredibly romantic *orangerie* on our way.

"Would you happen to know the estate's annual upkeep cost?" I ask.

He shakes his head.

"Can you ask your friend? I'll need that info to determine the price."

"I'll be sure to get you that info within a day or two," he says, before adding, "It must cost a small fortune to keep an estate like that."

I nod. "Whoever buys this, had better have deep pockets. Or tap into the huge revenue potential of the estate."

"Paying guests?"

"Yes, among other things," I say. "If I were the owner, I'd immediately apply for permits to restore the chateau and convert one of the wings into a hotel."

"You think the historic monuments committee would allow it?"

"If the request is vetted by a good architect and shows how the new income-generating activities will fund the preservation works and the return of the castle to its former grandeur, I'm sure they will."

He gives me a sidelong look. "Do you have other *income-generating* activities in mind?"

"You bet!" I begin to unfold fingers on my left hand as I tick off ideas. "I'd rent out the great hall for receptions, and that huge central lawn for music festivals and events. I'd restart the winery. I'd set up a gift shop and hire a guide to do daily tours of the chateau—"

"We—," he cuts in, "I mean, Sebastian already allows guided tours of the grotto."

"Good," I say. "But clearly not enough."

We walk in silence for a few more minutes. The colors and shapes of this amazing estate regale my eyes. This place deserves so much more love than it's currently getting. Delicate floral scents fill the hazy midafternoon air, which become more pungent when we reach the vines.

"How many hectares?" I ask.

"Err…"

"I'll need that info, too."

He smiles. "*Oui, M'dame.*"

We stare at the rows of trellised plants.

"Are the castle's cellars big?" I ask.

"Very."

"And the equipment, do you think it's still there?"

"I'm sure it is."

"That's an additional source of income!" I grin, bubbling with enthusiasm. "The new owner could start a sort of cooperative winery. Small growers with no facilities of their own could rent space and equipment in the chateau's cellars. Even amateurs could pay to get their bespoke wines. That's how it's done in the US, especially in California."

Noah says nothing.

He's crouching among the vines, stroking their trunks and running his fingers along the shoots. Reverently, he caresses the leaves and gently cups a bulging, vibrant bunch of ripe grapes, as if weighing it in his hand. When he snaps off a juicy red grape and tosses it into his mouth, his lids drop and an expression of rapture appears on his face as he savors it.

He opens his eyes and surveys the plot, mumbling, "I didn't realize someone still tended these vines…"

"When were they planted?"

"Decades ago, by Sebastian's grandfather."

"Well, maybe your buddy Sebastian feels it's his duty to keep these vines alive."

Noah turns to me. "Maybe."

"Do you know if this vineyard is rated grand cru?"

"It is."

"Wow. Good for Sebastian—it adds huge value." I blow out a sigh. "I think he's mad to sell this."

"He needs—" Noah begins.

"Money," I finish for him. "I know, I know… But if I owned this estate, there'd be only one way it would change hands." I pause for effect. "Over my dead body."

He gives me a funny look. "How far would you go to get your hands on a property like this?"

"Far."

"Would you marry its current or future owner, even if you'd never met him and didn't have any feelings for him?"

"Feelings shmeelings." I say what I always say when Mom or Sue become too sentimental. "All they do is cloud your judgment and lead to disappointments down the road."

"Does that mean you'd marry him?"

Does it?

Oh, who cares—I'm just making a point.

"Duh," I say, rolling my eyes. "In a wink."

SEVENTEEN
Noah

"This is Hamlet and me age twenty-one." Juliet points at an old, photo in the big album on Sophie's lap. "This picture was taken in Beirut a few months after our wedding."

The women sit next to each other on the couch, looking at Juliet's family pictures. Hamlet and I lounge in roomy armchairs on either end of the coffee table.

Oscar and Cannelle have fallen asleep at our feet—Cannelle balled up on top of her favorite cushion and not making a sound like the gently bred lady she is. Oscar is lying on his back, hind legs wide open, and snoring happily. Being himself.

We're sipping post-dinner coffee from tiny cups. It was brewed Oriental-style which, according to Juliet, is "the only sensible way to drink coffee." While we're at it, we also wolf down a large number of small honey-soaked baklava.

The coffee was home-roasted, ground, and brewed by Hamlet. His lovely wife baked the baklavas. The Derzians know I'm not a big fan of desserts. *I* know that leaving their house without eating at least one baklava is simply not an option.

I crane my neck to look at the photo. Hamlet wears flared pants and a red shirt open down to his stomach to reveal a hairy chest. His hair is big and his mustache reminds me of Tom Selleck. Juliet is dressed in a ridiculously short skirt and platform shoes. Her long hair is parted in the middle. She wears a braided headband around her forehead.

Sophie gives our hostess a surprised look. "A miniskirt? In Lebanon?"

"Of course." Juliet shrugs. "Every self-respecting fashionista had one of those back in the day."

"You're the coolest hippie I've ever seen," Sophie says.

Juliet lets out a nostalgic sigh. "I used to have such pretty legs."

"Me, too," Hamlet echoes from his armchair, misty-eyed.

Sophie giggles.

Hamlet turns to his wife. "She thinks I'm kidding. Show her our Saint-Tropez pictures."

Juliet turns a few pages until she finds the Saint-Tropez pics. It's a series of four color photographs immortalizing the couple on the famed Riviera beach. Their bodies are fiercely tanned. Juliet is clad in a tiny, low-cut bikini. Hamlet stands next to his wife with an arm around her shoulders, proudly hairy everywhere with only a tiny scrap of bright blue fabric covering his boy parts.

My water polo Speedo would qualify as conservative next to Hamlet's Chippendales outfit.

I open my mouth to thank God that the Borat-style mankini wasn't invented until this century, when he gives me a narrow-eyed *don't-you-dare* look.

"It's true," I say. "Both of you have pretty legs."

Hamlet turns to Sophie. "Told you."

"You're a beautiful couple," Sophie says.

Juliet smiles. "We were destined for each other, and not just because we both had Shakespearean names. We were born the same year and our mothers were best friends."

"That's a good start." I grab the chance to give an outlet to my censored sarcasm. "But from there to call it *destiny…*"

Hamlet leans in. "When I proposed to Juliet for the first time, I dropped to my knees and asked her to be my wife before God and man."

"I said 'no way,' " Juliet says.

Hamlet nods. "My heart sank. Had I been blind? Could it be that Juliet didn't love me the way I loved her? So I asked her, my voice trembling, 'Why not?' "

He marks a pause.

I glance at Juliet, expecting her to pick up the tale, but she gazes at her husband, clearly unwilling to interfere with his show.

"What did she say?" Sophie asks.

Hamlet waits a few more seconds before answering. "She said, 'Because proposing on both knees is lame.' "

Sophie gasps at such extreme shallowness and turns to Juliet. "Really?"

Juliet nods.

"What did you do?" I ask Hamlet.

"What else was I supposed to do?" He shrugs. "I rearranged myself in the proper kneeling position and asked her to marry me again."

Sophie smiles. "And she said yes, right?"

"She said no."

I wonder why this time. Was he too poor for her liking? A cabinetmaker with no connections and no family money, did she believe he wasn't good enough for her? Was she hoping to snag a sheik or, failing that, a wealthy *homme d'affaires*?

A smile turns up the corners of Hamlet's lips. "I asked her why not again. She rolled her eyes and said, 'Because we're twelve, silly.' "

Sophie bursts out laughing.

I chuckle, too, absurdly relieved.

"I proposed again when we were eighteen," Hamlet says, grinning.

Juliet smoothes her hair back. "I said yes, but I made him wait two more years until we turned twenty."

Hamlet reaches over and pats her hand. "You were totally worth the wait, sweetheart."

Sophie and I thank our hosts and stand up.

"She's a keeper," Juliet whispers in my ear while she cheek kisses me good-bye. "Don't mess it up, boy."

I think of all the omissions, half-truths, and outright lies I've fed Sophie about who I am and where I come from, and my stomach knots.

It's quite possible I've already messed it up.

EIGHTEEN
Sophie

Noah opens the door and glances at his watch. "We're back home and it's only nine. Three cheers for same-landing dinner parties."

"I like your neighbors," I say.

He smiles. "You might like them less next time when Juliet will keep you hostage until you've seen her children's albums. An album per child per year."

"Why didn't she do it this time?"

"She knows I have an important game tomorrow, so she took pity."

Tomorrow, Noah, Zach, and the rest of the team are playing the first national championship game of the season against *Olympique Toulon*. The game will be in Paris. And Noah gave me a premium ticket.

"See?" I say. "Your neighbors *are* lovely and they really like you."

"They really like Oscar."

"Him, too, but if I didn't know, I'd assume they were your family."

Noah's expression grows bleak, and he quickly crouches to pet Oscar. Clearly, he doesn't like to talk or even be reminded about his family. Since we met, I've told him tons about my mom, my dad, my friends, and my childhood. He's told me almost nothing. I've pieced together that he grew up in Burgundy and later in Nepal where he hung out with Uma before returning to France. His mom stayed back in Nepal. He loves her. His father died years ago, I'm not sure from what. Noah hates him because he refused to help his ex-wife and his son when they were in a tight spot.

That's about it, really.

Could Noah be embarrassed by his modest origins? He doesn't strike me as a status seeker, and he talks about his pizza delivery job without a problem. Not that he talks about it much. The only things he's always happy to discuss are Oscar and water polo. And maybe the Derzians—at least, until my uncalled-for comment.

I chide myself for being so gauche, but when he nudges Oscar toward his crate and stands up, there's no unease or hesitation in his eyes.

Uh-oh. It looks like someone remembered the plans we made for tonight.

Noah runs the tips of his fingers over my cheeks, jawline and lips, featherlight. "Are we still on?"

I nod, taking deep breaths so I won't tremble.

He steps back and scoops me up into his arms and carries me to the bedroom.

I ask him to pause as soon as we're inside and pull the door shut behind us. When my feet touch the floor, I decide I'm going to be adventurous. I know I can trust Noah not to hurt me. He'll stop the moment I say stop. Granted, I haven't known him very long, but I know the important part. The part that matters, the part that defines him.

Noah wants me, but he won't let his desire control his actions. After all, I spent two nights in his arms without him trying to cajole me to have sex or—worse—force himself on me. And without me having to say no more than once.

You can do it, Sophie!

Tentatively, I cup his bulge through his jeans.

Surprise flashes in his eyes before his face relaxes into a satisfied grin. "Just so you know, I totally approve of the way you're going about this."

"Shut up and unbuckle that belt," I say, settling into my brand-new seductress persona.

He executes.

I undo his jeans and slowly push them, together with his underwear, down his narrow hips and muscled thighs. He loses his T while I'm at it. When he's stark naked, I zero in on his proud manhood and touch it. Reveling in the wonderful contrast between the warm, velvety skin and the hardness it encases, I run my fingers up and down before wrapping them around him.

His flesh throbs against my palm.

My core grows heavy in response, pulling, aching for him.

Suddenly, his hands are everywhere. Noah unbuttons, unclasps and pulls my clothes off, stroking every part he uncovers. All the while I keep pressing my palm against his length, letting go of it only for two brief moments so he can strip my bra and shirt away.

He rakes my bared body with a scorching gaze. Then he bends down, his mouth closing over my right nipple and his big hand cupping my breast. His other hand rubs my belly and slides between my legs.

Ooh, it's welcome there. So very welcome.

Noah's gaze is scalding when he lifts his head and stares into my eyes. "You're dripping wet for me."

"So are you," I say, running the pad of my thumb over his tip.

He grins.

I give him a satisfied smirk. Who knew Frigid Sophie had a sex kitten in her?

Suddenly, Noah lets go of me and jumps onto the bed. The next moment he's flat on his back, a condom in his hand. "Come here."

I climb on the bed and sit on my heels next to him.

He rolls the condom on and lays a hand on my hip. "Ride me?"

That's not quite how I expected him to initiate our first full-blown lovemaking, but I'm game. I straddle his hips and begin to lower myself on him, very slowly, listening to my body's reactions. There's no trace of pain, no discomfort—just pleasure. Noah's hands are on my hips, hot and strong, but he isn't trying to accelerate my descent by pushing me down. Nor does he lift his hips.

When I'm fully impaled, I wiggle a little, loving the feel of him inside me. He thrusts tentatively. I push down to meet him.

Soon, we establish a rhythm, moving in perfect synch.

"*Bébé,*" he rasps after a while. "I can't hold out much longer."

I bend over him and kiss his lips. "That's OK. I don't know if I can come like this, anyway."

His expression is still hesitant, so I add, "But I've *really* enjoyed this ride."

He nods, and tightens his grip on my hips. I let him lift me up a little and hold me steady where he wants me. His thrusts come faster, harder, the cadence accelerating to frantic. A minute later, his face contorts and he groans his pleasure.

I climb off him.

He turns on his side and puts his hand on my mound. There's a question in his eyes.

"Yes, please," I say.

He begins to caress, varying the amount of pressure and the pace, asking me if he should move left or right, go faster or slow down. Inhibited as I am about dirty talk, his simple questions make it incredibly easy to guide him, coaxing more and more joy from his hand.

Something begins to build inside me, and then I come, gasping at the sweetness of the release.

When the last wave of pleasure subsides, I turn to Noah. "Good job."

"Sorry you didn't get a vaginal orgasm." He strokes my upper arm, before resting his hand on my shoulder. "I was hoping we'd come together."

I blink. "Are you kidding me? I've just had *penetration*, and I enjoyed it. I *loved* it. You have no idea what that means to me."

He smiles. "Tell me."

"It means I can stop lying to myself that being frigid is great, that frigidity rocks, because it gives you protection against dumb choices."

"It doesn't?" he asks with fake innocence.

I roll my eyes. "Only death gives you protection against dumb choices. All frigidity has *really* given me so far is a feeling I was missing out on a lot of fun and on an important part of human experience. A feeling that I was… defective."

"You're perfect, *bébé*," he says.

I give him a mischievous smile. "Maybe I am now that you've untwisted my vagina."

His grin becomes so big I fear the corners of his mouth might crack.

Pressing a hot kiss to its left side and then the right, I add, "This *bébé* will always be grateful for that, Noah Masson, no matter how things end between us."

When I find my seat on the deck level, Uma and Sam are already there. Uma is armed with blue pom-poms and Sam, a blue foam hand. Sam is wearing a jersey with a big three on the front. I imagine it's Zach's number.

"Hey!" Uma greets me with a bear hug. "I'm glad you made it. This is going to be fun."

Her warmth and genuine friendliness make it hard to resent her, and yet I do. For what she means to Noah. For the possibility of their future together and even for their shared memories.

Why couldn't this Himalayan rose be less sweet? Or less pretty?

Thirty minutes later, the game is in full swing, and the three of us are cheering our heads off. Noah's team is winning. All the white caps seem to be in top form, but Noah's and Zach's play is wicked. By the second quarter, Zach has scored four goals and Noah has saved as many. He's on fire. I can see now what he meant when he told me about the importance of a big arm span, strong hands, and "explosiveness" in the goal cage.

And he's cunning.

Time after time, I watch the goalie of *Nageurs de Paris* lure Toulon*'s* attackers into aiming at the side of the goal cage he's left unprotected. Only he hasn't. The moment they take the bait and shoot, he leaps out of the water and blocks the shot with an incredible precision.

It's also fun watching him get all bossy and bark at the defense players to move left or right, keep their eyes on the ball, or slow down a specific attacker.

The commentator raves about Noah.

"Tremendous save by the goalkeeper!"

"Strong hands!"

"Noah Masson continues his amazing set of saves!"

"Goalkeeper did well—what a fabulous stop!"

The man is in love.

Unfortunately, Toulon's players are just as inspired as the Parisians, if not more. They dominate the field, shooting so often and in such a perfectly coordinated and well-practiced way that they net the ball as often as the Parisians, even with Noah guarding the goal.

At the very end of the final quarter, one of the Parisian players commits a major foul, and Toulon sets up for a penalty. Everyone in the audience holds their breath. Noah explained to me that a water polo penalty shot is so hard to stop, it's almost always a sure goal. And to make matters worse, the score is tied. If Toulon scores, they win the match.

The attacker takes his time preparing, and then fakes a shot. Noah hardly budges, his eyes glued to the ball. After two more fakes, the real shot comes, powerful and precise. I brace for the worst.

Noah blocks with his head, rushes to the ball, catches it, swims forward, and passes it to a teammate. The player passes it on to Zach, who slams it into Toulon's cage.

Everyone freezes, watching the trajectory of the yellow ball as if in slow motion. The second it flies above the goalie's hand and hits the net, the arena roars with excitement.

"What a save!" the commentator shrieks. "What a shot! Unbelievable!" He chokes on his delight and begins to cough.

The white caps cheer and throw up their arms, fists clenched. It's over. Time to pop the bubbly.

Nageurs de Paris won.

NINETEEN
Noah

Nageurs de Paris opened the season with a win against *Olympique Toulon* and went on to defeat three more clubs—on their home turf, as it were.

Today we played in Paris again, trouncing Aix-en-Provence, 14–6. Lucas is very happy. As per our recently established tradition, he's treating all his men, together with their partners and children, to celebratory drinks. We've already finished the requisite bottle of champagne and switched to beer, wine, and sodas for the kids.

All four of them are having a blast at the moment with a silly game organized by Denis.

He's placed four small paper bags on the floor—one for each kid—and has them take turns at picking theirs up with their mouths. They aren't allowed to touch the bag, or the floor, with their hands. When they fail, Denis asks them to jump on one leg while singing. When one of them succeeds, Denis picks up his scissors and cuts a centimeter or two from the top of that kid's bag.

"What's the point of this game?" Uma asks him.

"The one with the shortest bag when I say stop, wins." Denis smiles. "Want to play?"

Turns out she does, and so do Sophie, Zach, and all the other adults in our group.

When the children are done, we line up by the wall and look at Denis.

"What's the prize?" Julien asks.

Denis pulls a small bag of gummy bears from his backpack.

Jean-Michel stares. "Seriously?"

"I'd planned this for the kids, remember?" Denis shrugs before scratching his head. "Hmm... I got only one more paper bag."

We wait for him to find a miracle solution.

"OK," he says. "Different rules for grown-ups. This will be an elimination contest. If you pick up the bag when your turn comes, you stay and I crop it. If you fail, you're out."

Over the next forty-five minutes the café's patrons witness a competition almost as fierce as the one we just had in the pool. Only this time it's every man for himself.

Lucas is the first to be eliminated, followed by Jean-Michel and his girlfriend, Valentin, Julien, Denis's wife, Uma, Zach and the others. Sophie and I are the last *men* standing.

The bag barely rises above the floorboards now.

Valentin moves from one eliminated contender to the next, taking bets. Sophie gives me a mischievous look and begins to circle around the bag, swinging her arms to encourage cheers.

"Go Sophie!" Zach shouts.

"Traitor," I mouth to him.

Only I'm the traitor, seeing as I've stolen his would-be girlfriend. And he's being remarkably gracious about it.

Sophie rolls up her sleeves and does a few ear-to-shoulder stretches. "Fifteen years of beach yoga, people!"

The masses cheer.

She waits for them to go quiet before adding, "Four years of cheerleading!"

The audience chants her name.

"Heading to the top, U-S-A!" she chants, launching her fists in the air.

Watching her enjoy herself like this, completely uninhibited and infectiously exuberant, is a pure joy. If I wasn't her opponent, I'd be cheering her at the top of my voice.

But as it is, I have to defend the Tricolor.

I strike a bodybuilder pose exhibiting my biceps. "*Vive la* France!"

"Go Noah!" Uma hollers.

I put my hand over my heart and drop my head in recognition of her support.

"*Mesdames, Messieurs,*" Denis says, taking on a commentator's voice. "We are about to witness the final round of this tournament. A battle of the titans. A battle of civilizations! Eagle versus rooster. Doughnut versus croissant. Marilyn Monroe versus Brigitte Bardot. Elvis—"

"Get on with it," someone cuts in.

"All right, all right!" Denis turns to Sophie. "Your turn."

She plants her feet wide, entwines her fingers behind her back and starts lowering her torso with almost no visible effort. God, she's bendy! She sure wasn't lying about yoga and cheerleading.

Hmm, I wonder why she never mentioned either of those to me.

We may still be in a gray zone between dating and a relationship, but what we have is definitely more than casual sex. Or am I getting ahead of myself? After all, Sophie still has her life plan, and I'm probably just a fun distraction on her "Parisian holiday." The man who "untwisted" her vagina.

Maybe that's why she hasn't told me about her yoga and cheerleading passions.

Unless it's because I haven't been forthcoming about my own life, either.

Thing is, I'm not ready to tell her the truth yet. But I certainly want to know more about her. I'd like to hear what it was like growing up in Key West, I want to know what books and movies she likes, where she stands politically.

And I wouldn't mind a private demo of her yoga skills.

In fact, I'll ask for one tonight.

In bed.

My cock twitches when I picture Sophie arranging her gorgeous body in one particular posture.

"Dude, it's your turn now," Denis's voice snaps my attention back to the present moment.

Squatting in front of the bag, I try to grab it with my mouth—and fail.

Denis strides toward Sophie, takes her hand, and yanks it high. "Elastic Girl is the winner!"

Sophie jumps up and down, shouting, "Woohoo! Take that, frog-eaters!"

My phone rings in my pocket with Maman's ringtone. She must calling to ask about the result of the game.

I excuse myself and step out of the bar.

"Did you win?" Maman asks.

"Yes, we did."

"Congratulations!"

"Thanks, Maman." I hesitate. "Can I call you back tomorrow? I'm out celebrating with the team."

"Is Uma there, too?" she asks.

"Yes."

"What about that American woman you've been enthusing over lately? Is she there, too?"

"Yes. Why?"

"Are you dating her?"

"Yes."

Keeping this from Maman is pointless. Just as is keeping pretty much anything from her. Sooner or later, she'll find out, and she'll be upset. We don't want that.

When Maman is upset, she becomes emotionally unstable and gets horrible migraines. A couple of times she's even had suicidal thoughts. The one time I upset her *seriously*, she filled the bathtub with hot water, wrote a farewell note to me, and was about to set her plan in motion, when I came home from school.

At the regular time.

Is it unkind of me to think she hadn't actually meant to kill herself? Anyway, I've learned over the years to avoid doing things that would upset her.

Maman is silent for a long moment. I don't need to see her face to know she's rattled. Uma is the girl she's always wanted me to be with.

That was my intention, too.

But not anymore.

"I'll be in France next week," she finally says.

"Cool."

"I've decided to attend Raphael and Mia's wedding."

"Really?"

"Yes. Did you get their invite?"

"I tossed it in the trash, same as their engagement party invite, Lily's christening party invite, and all other RSVPs I've been receiving from the d'Arcys."

She doesn't comment.

"I'm surprised you're going," I say.

"So am I, but... Since Raphael visited me last year, I've done a lot of thinking."

"And?"

She sighs audibly. "He was too young at the time. We cannot hold him responsible for sticking with his older brother who'd been a father figure to him ever since his Papa engaged on the path of debauchery."

"That may very well be, but—"

"You should go, too. For my sake. I'd like you and Raphael to make up."

What?

"You don't have to decide right now," she says quickly. "Go back to your friends, and we'll discuss this in person in three days."

When I return to the bar, Sophie is sipping her wine at the long table. I sit down next to her.

She offers me a gummy bear. "No hard feelings?"

"None." I turn to her. "You won fair and square."

She beams.

I take the candy from her hand. "Thank you for sharing the bounty."

"How's your mom?"

"Fine," I say. "She's coming to Paris next week."

I almost add "for my middle brother's wedding" before remembering I've never mentioned a middle brother to Sophie. Or any brother, for that matter.

My lovely girlfriend shifts in her chair to face me. "Tell me something. Why did you leave Nepal two years ago?"

"So I could join a good water polo club and play professionally."

It's what I always say when asked that question.

"Oh yeah, I remember!" She smiles. "Nepalis are more into elephant polo than water polo, right?"

"Yep."

But not quite.

On those rare occasions when I look into my soul, I see a more complex answer. There's the water polo, of course, but there's also… Maman. The truth is, regardless of all my love for her and my admiration for what she does, I needed a break. I needed to put some distance—more precisely, a dozen countries and a couple of seas—between us.

Sophie offers me another gummy bear.

I open my mouth and she feeds it to me. Unable to resist the temptation, I kiss the tips of her fingers. She stares into my eyes, biting her lower lip.

Suddenly, nothing else matters. All I want is to be alone with her in my bedroom. Or in her bedroom. Or anywhere we won't be disturbed. With no match to play tomorrow, not even a practice session in the morning—Lucas has given us two days off—I'm planning to pleasure her until she begs me to stop. Judging by the way she's looking at me right now, she won't object to my plan.

Sophie's purse rings.

She pulls out her phone and gives me an apologetic smile. "It's Dad. I better answer it."

While she's outside, I go over to Uma and Sam. The boy declares that I played well, but I'm not as good as his dad who's the best player in the world. Uma grins and ruffles his hair. Nodding in agreement, I look around for Zach. He's sitting at the other end of the table, half listening to Julien talk about something animatedly.

His eyes are trained on Uma.

If I didn't know Zach better, I'd say he's leering.

But I must be wrong.

Zach is the ultimate gentleman, and Uma is an ingénue from a very conservative background with no family in France. She's his employee. And his teammate's best friend. Those are lines he won't cross, if I know him at all.

Zach blinks as if waking up from a trance and says something to Julien.

I turn back to Sam and Uma, shamefaced. My sick mind must've misread Zach's expression. He's overprotective of his son. No doubt it's Sam he was staring at—not Uma.

When Sophie returns, her smile is strained.

"Something wrong?" I ask.

"No." She gives me a funny look. "Dad's here in Paris. I'm sorry, but I have to go home."

TWENTY
Sophie

Dad lets go of me after the longest hug in Bander family history. No wonder, considering this has been our longest time apart.

"I hope you haven't had dinner yet," he says petting my braids. "I booked a table downstairs."

Downstairs must be the hotel's restaurant.

What with all the drinks and gummy bears I've consumed this afternoon, I'm not hungry, but I won't ruin Dad's evening by saying no to his invitation.

"At what time?"

"About now."

"Great," I say. "Let's go."

"So, how do you like living and working in Paris?" Dad asks once we're seated.

I smile. "A lot."

He doesn't look pleased to hear that.

"Sophie," he says in a tone that bodes nothing good for me. "I won't beat about the bush. I'm concerned."

"Is that why you flew in?"

He nods.

I poke and push my food around the plate, waiting for Dad to continue.

"How's Catherine?" he asks instead.

Stalling, eh? "Mom's doing great. She got the post she's been vying for, so she's happy."

"Good," he says. "Is she seeing someone?"

I lift my eyes from my plate. Dad wears his poker face, but I detect emotion in his eyes and a bit of anxiety in his voice.

Interesting. "No," I say. "She isn't. Why are you asking?"

"Just curious."

Don't read too much into this, Sophie.

They've been divorced almost a decade, and I've lost count of false alarms and broken dreams of their reunification. It just isn't happening.

Mom loves her movie critic's job, especially now that she got hired by the biggest daily in the country. When she lived with us in Key West and Dad called her Cat, she submitted movie reviews to dozens, maybe hundreds of periodicals, but her English wasn't good enough to allow her to express herself with the same witty elegance she does in French. She landed other jobs—and hated them. She tried to be a stay-at-home mom and hated that, too. She missed her parents and friends. And she loathed the Keys weather ten months out of twelve.

While Dad's business expanded and took more and more of his time with every passing year, Mom became increasingly withdrawn and sad. Her doctor gave her antidepressants, but they didn't seem to help much. With hindsight, I don't think Mom was depressed. She just never managed to make Key West her home.

When I turned fourteen, she announced she had to go back to France or she'd go crazy. She begged Dad to follow her. He refused.

The rows they had that year! He'd tell her she was capricious and irresponsible to ask him to abandon a flourishing business and uproot me just because she didn't like the fucking weather. She'd call him self-centered and unfeeling, since he couldn't see it was a matter of survival for her.

After months and months of arguments, they finally agreed to disagree. Mom was returning to France, Dad was staying put, and I was asked to choose.

Talk about impossible choices.

In the end, I stayed with Dad. It wasn't just about picking him over Mom. It was choosing what I knew and cherished over the unknown. I loved my school and my friends, our big house on Elizabeth Street, the shows on TV, the cheerleading, the beach...

"Your daughter?" someone at the table on our left asks Dad, breaking me from my reminiscences.

A stylish woman in her mid-forties is looking from me to Dad.

He nods.

The woman gives Dad a coquettish smile. "Stunning, just like her dad."

I take a closer look at her. Blonde, fit and well groomed, she's clearly flirting with Dad. Her friend, a plump brunette of about the same age is scrutinizing Dad's hands for a wedding band.

I smile politely, struggling not to roll my eyes.

This happens all the time. Dad gets hit on by women of all ages, colors, and sizes. He's held up well—in fact, *very* well—but it's not just that. He has that Denzel Washington air about him—poised and strong with the tiniest hint of intensity and an even tinier smile hiding in the corner of his mouth.

It wreaks havoc with women's brains.

The funny thing is he doesn't seem to care. Since the divorce, he's had a dozen dates and a couple of short-lived relationships, but nothing serious. When I ask him, he says he has no time and he's already married—to his job.

"Thank you," he says to the blonde and turns away without a second glance.

I search his face. "Spit it out, Dad. What are you so concerned about that you flew all the way here, abandoning ship at a busy time?"

He studies his food for a moment before he looks me in the eye. "I worry that you'll decide to stay here at the end of your internship."

"What makes you think that?"

"The way you speak about that *boy*, Noah Masson."

"The *boy* is twenty-seven," I say. "And you're totally overreacting. It's just a summer fling... er, summer and fall fling. I haven't changed my plans."

"Yet," he says. "You haven't changed them *yet*. But I can see it coming a mile away. You've never sounded so... into someone before. In fact, you've never *been* into someone before."

I wave my hand dismissively. "Let's not jump to conclusions."

He sighs. "Anyhow. The other reason I'm in France is that I'm invited to a high-society wedding next weekend. Will you accompany me?"

I arch an eyebrow. "I didn't know you had high-society connections here."

"I have many connections in many places that you aren't aware of," he says. "So will you come? I wouldn't want to go alone."

"Sure. I'll keep you company, Dad. It'll be my chance to wear that big-ticket gown I brought with me and never had an opportunity to show off."

"The one you wore to your graduation? I love that gown," Dad says.

"Me, too."

When we're done, he walks me to Mom's where I'll be sleeping over tonight. My place is farther away, and Noah's is across the city. Besides, it would be too awkward asking Dad to put me in a cab so I can spend the night with a man. A man he clearly disapproves of.

Luckily for me, Mom doesn't.

"I've never seen you so into someone before," she says at some point in our now-traditional kitchen table confab.

Funny how she gives a positive spin to the words Dad had uttered with horror earlier tonight.

"It may turn out to be nothing," I say.

"Sure. But it may also turn out to be something beautiful and lasting. You have to let it blossom."

"Dad worries I'll give up on my future to be with Noah."

Mom says nothing.

"Isn't that what *you* did?" I ask, before adding, "And regretted it?"

She takes a heavy breath. "I never regretted marrying your dad, or having you. It's just… I know how much you and Ludwig love Key West, but that place was slowly killing me."

I take her hand over the table and give it a squeeze. "I'm sorry, Mom. I didn't mean to—"

"I saw Ludwig earlier today," she says, interrupting me.

"You did?"

They haven't met in ages.

"The years have been kind to him," she says, smiling.

"So have they been to you."

"That's what Ludwig seems to think, too." She pushes a strand behind her ear. "He said I looked just as smashing as when he first laid eyes on me."

I can't believe my ears—or my eyes. "Mom, you're blushing."

"No I'm not. Anyway, it doesn't mean anything."

I cock my head. "What's the deal? Did he just show up on your doorstep?"

She laughs. "Nothing so dramatic. He called and said he was in Paris in a hotel not far from me and asked if I wanted to have a coffee for old times' sake."

I wait for her to tell me more about their *coffee*, but she changes the topic.

As I listen to her talk about the latest movie she saw and the review she was writing for it, I can't help wondering if my parents still have feelings for each other.

The other thing I wonder about is whose hunch about Noah will carry the day. Will our fling turn into something more? Will I change my plans and stay in France so I can be with him? Or will he be willing to move to Key West to be with me?

Sheesh.

I should learn to live in the present moment, and stop building castles in the sky.

They're known to crumble at the slightest puff of wind.

TWENTY-ONE
Noah

"When will you come over again?" Sam asks me.

"In a couple of weeks." I scoop him up and sit him on my lap at the garden table.

Uma comes out of the house carrying a tray loaded with three glasses of iced water and three bowls of ice cream—regular for her and me, and a special homemade concoction for Sam. After an hour of playing tag, this is just what we need.

"Is it normal for late October to be so warm in Paris?" she asks.

"No, this is much warmer than the norm." I ruffle Sam's soft curls. "Your dad and I are playing two major tournaments this season, so we'll be away quite a bit."

He nods, a solemn look on his face. "I know."

Uma sits down across from us and gives Sam a wink. "I'll arrange a bunch of playdates with your chums Evan and Mo while your dad and Noah are traveling."

Sam's eyes light up.

"Besides," Uma says. "I have some outings planned for us."

The boy's eyes are sparkling now. "To the movies?"

"Yes, but not only." Uma leans in. "We're also going to the zoo and to the circus."

Sam jumps off my lap, bounds around the table, and wraps his arms around Uma.

She kisses the top of his head. "Listen, why don't you watch a couple of *Diego* episodes, while Noah and I discuss some boring grown-up stuff?"

He grabs his bowl and scoots into the house.

Uma points at the untouched water he left behind and sighs. "He's got his priorities straight... Hang on."

She picks up the glass and carries it into the house. Through the open window, I hear her negotiate with Sam around ice cream, water, and Diego.

When she returns, I ask her about her embroidery school. She says she's learning a lot and loving every moment of it.

"Good." I smile and point my chin to the house. "It looks like you're not too unhappy about your part-time job, either."

She beams. "Sam is the sweetest kid I've ever met."

"How is it going with Zach?"

"Fine." She looks down at her ice cream bowl.

"Uma?" I narrow my eyes. "Is there something you want to tell me?"

She shakes her head before lifting her eyes to me. "But I have a question for you."

I lean in. "Shoot."

"Is Sophie still in the dark about who you are?"

Not quite the question I expected. I nod.

"Why?" she asks.

"It's complicated."

She scowls.

I duck my head in mock panic.

She lays her hands on the table. "I get it that you don't want to be associated with the d'Arcys, and you don't want strangers to know your real name. I respect that. But you did tell Zach. Why not confide in Sophie, too? I'm sure your secret will be safe with her."

This is awkward.

Uma may be an innocent, but she's far from stupid. I'm sure she's figured out by now that Sophie and I have become more than friends. Does it bother her? If she's still in love with me, I don't see how it wouldn't. Yet, she seems to genuinely like Sophie and believes she deserves my honesty, which my girlfriend totally does.

"You're right," I say. "As a matter of fact, I've decided to come clean with her next time I see her."

Hopefully next week, what with her father having monopolized her free time.

Uma lets out a relieved sigh. "Good decision."

We sit in silence for a moment.

"Did you go to Raphael's rehearsal dinner?" I ask. "Maman told me she was taking you along."

Uma slaps her forehead. "I was going to tell you about it! Can't believe it's been a week already..." She shakes her head. "Time clearly moves faster here than in Nepal."

"Definitely," I say.

She tilts her head to the side. "Are you coming to the wedding tomorrow?"

"No."

"You should."

"Did Maman put you up to this?" I lean my elbows on the table and rub my face. "She keeps saying Raphael can't be blamed for Sebastian's choices."

"Marguerite is right." Uma takes a breath. "Anyway, I really enjoyed myself except for a bit of weirdness at one point."

I raise my eyebrows.

"I overheard a conversation." She shifts uncomfortably. "Someone called Marguerite when we were hanging out on the patio. After she asked who was calling, she just listened for a long time, and then..."

Uma falls silent, hesitating.

"What did she say?" I prompt.

"She said she was thrilled to hear their interests were aligned. She asked whoever was calling to let her think about it and she'd call him back."

"Probably a potential donor."

"That's what I thought, too." Uma gives me a funny look. "But when she phoned that person back a few minutes later, she said, 'I'll call you tonight to explain the details, but if my plan works, you'll return to Florida with your daughter'."

I gasp.

Was her caller Sophie's dad? Have they joined forces in plotting to separate us? That would explain his sudden visit and keeping Sophie busy every evenings with various activities.

I glance at Uma. She looks like she's about to burst into tears.

"What's wrong?" I ask.

"I shouldn't've told you." She wrings her wrists. "Marguerite has always been so kind to me, and I feel like I'm betraying her… It's just that what she's doing is wrong… and unfair to you and Sophie."

I give her a long stare. "Uma, I must be blunt here. Aren't your interests aligned with Maman's and Sophie's father's? Don't you want Sophie to go away?"

She blinks. "Why would I? She makes you happy—it's obvious. And I'm your friend."

A light bulb goes off in my head.

Uma isn't in love with me. It's been Maman's wishful thinking the whole time. She saw something that wasn't there, and she made me see it, too, through her sheer will and power of persuasion. Because she wanted her favorite son to marry her chosen protégée.

That's just so Marguerite.

She is all about benevolence, only her benevolence comes at a price—control over the lives of those she cares for.

"Oh, my God!" Uma claps a hand to her mouth. "You think I'm in love with you."

"I—"

She shakes her head. "Of course you would. I'm sure that's what Marguerite has told you."

I close my eyes for a moment, thinking. "Has Maman told *you* that you're in love with me?"

"Yes, a million times. And that you're the reason I came to France."

"And I'm not."

She shakes her head. "It was for the embroidery school. And to escape an arranged marriage without my parents' losing face."

I run my hand through my hair. "Did Maman tell you *I* was in love with you?"

She nods.

My jaw clenches.

"Don't worry." Uma smiles. "I never bought it. You do love me, I'm sure, but only as a friend. I've never caught you looking at me the way you look at Sophie, or the way… other men look at me."

"For the record," I say, "I've never caught *you* looking at me that way, either."

She smiles.

We sit in silence for a long moment and then I stand up. "I better tell Sophie the truth before her dad does it."

Uma nods. "And, please, come to Raphael's wedding."

"I will."

If not to make up with my brothers, then to confront Maman.

TWENTY-TWO
Sophie

As I admire the wedding venue, which is a sumptuous *hôtel particulier* in the heart of Paris, I wish I had my phone to take a selfie. I would send it to Noah, just to show off. Only, my phone has gone missing since yesterday lunchtime. I've turned the office and my apartment upside down, and called myself from Dad's phone multiple times, but nada.

It was probably stolen from my purse during lunch.

I'm not too upset, though. All my data is backed up on the cloud, and the phone was an old model with a cracked screen. Dad announced he was buying me the newest and coolest model tomorrow. Because he feels guilty. Beats me how choosing the restaurant where my phone got stolen makes it his fault, but hey, if Mr. Bander needs a pretext to pamper his *princess*, I won't stand in his way.

The *maître d'hotel* directs us to the patio where pre-dinner drinks and sophisticated-looking snacks are being served. I understand the church wedding was held yesterday, in Alsace, where the bride's mother is a pastor. It was only family and closest friends. This morning, a bigger ceremony was held at the town hall of their arrondissement, and now it's the dinner party for a much larger circle.

Which—lo and behold—includes Dad and me.

A good-looking French woman in her fifties approaches us with an adorable little girl in her arms.

"Ludwig! I'm so glad you could make it." She tilts her head toward the baby. "This is Lily, my granddaughter, courtesy of the newlyweds."

Dad points to me. "This is my daughter, Sophie."

"Pleased to meet you, Sophie," the woman says. "I'm Marguerite."

Noah's mom is called Marguerite, too. Must have been a fashionable name for that generation.

I smile. "*Enchantée.* And congratulations on your son's wedding!"

"Thank you, darling." She looks at Dad. "I'm happy to be here, but I'm also anxious to get back to work."

"I know what you mean," he says.

She turns to me. "I run a charitable foundation. The manager and staff are perfectly competent, and yet… You see, I'm a very hands-on philanthropist."

She smiles and eyes me up and down.

"*Magnifique,*" she says to Dad, giving him a meaningful look.

His nod is cursory but just as meaningful. "Yes, she is."

Why do I get a feeling they've included me in some game they're playing without explaining the rules?

"Have you met Raphael and Mia yet?" Marguerite asks.

I follow her gaze to the stunning couple surrounded by a group of guests across the room.

"Not yet," I say. "But I'm looking forward to it."

A boyishly pretty young woman with a professional camera around her neck, is walking toward us. A step behind her is a handsome albeit aloof man holding a baby boy in his arms.

"Will you excuse me for a moment?" Marguerite gives us a perfunctory smile and scoots off.

The woman with the camera halts next to us. "Hi, I'm Diane, the unofficial photographer of this wedding."

She holds out her hand.

I shake it.

"*Chéri*," she says to the man holding the baby. "Will you and Tanguy stand over there for a quick pic?"

The man goes to the designated spot and poses.

When she's done, Diane turns to me again. "I hope we can chat later, when I'm done with my official and unofficial duties."

The stiff man passes the baby to a middle-aged woman—a nanny, I guess—who takes him out to the garden.

He extends his hand. "Sebastian d'Arcy."

I shake it, after which he shakes hands with Dad.

Dad turns to me. "This young man is Count Sebastian d'Arcy du Grand-Thouars de Saint-Maurice, owner of one of the most successful businesses in Europe."

I've never seen a count—or any aristocrat—before.

Am I supposed to *curtsy?*

Nah. He isn't the Queen of England, after all.

Weird how Dad stressed the man's title and fancy name. Is he so impressed he forgot he's American, and a *conch* to top it off? In Key West, we aren't given to formalities. Dad usually calls everyone by their nickname, regardless of status or position.

Something else bugs me.

It's the last part of count d'Arcy's long name. For some reason, those words sounded familiar... Wait a minute! The chateau Noah took me to in September was called Thouars-Maurice. And its owner was called Sebastian. This cannot be a coincidence. No effing way. Count d'Arcy du Grand-Thouars de Saint-Maurice is Noah's buddy Sebastian.

Fancy that!

"I visited your amazing estate last month," I say to him with a smile.

His eyebrows rise from which I deduce Noah hasn't told him he'd asked me to give him a hand selling the property.

Then again, why would he? It's not like either of us is getting a commission.

Count d'Arcy opens his mouth as if to say something, shuts it, and gives me a polite smile. "I'm glad you liked it. The estate is my brother's, actually."

"Raphael's?"

"No, my *other* brother's."

Curiouser and curiouser.

I'm sure Noah said the owner of the estate was his friend Sebastian, not his friend Sebastian's brother. But why on earth would he lie about it? Why would anyone bother lying about such an unimportant, minor detail?

I must've misunderstood.

But why didn't he mention his friend was a count? Probably because Sebastian's title doesn't mean anything to Noah. It doesn't define Sebastian in Noah's eyes.

Fair enough.

What I really can't explain is why Noah told me his friend was in need of cash, when Sebastian d'Arcy clearly isn't.

Maybe Sebastian's *other* brother is. I'll have to ask Noah—

Who's right here, barely a dozen feet from me, chatting with the bride. And with Uma.

What is he doing here? What is Uma doing here?

D'oh! This is his friend's brother's wedding. Noah was *invited.*

And he chose to come here with Uma.

"Excuse me," I say to Dad and Sebastian, and begin making my way toward Noah.

"So, should I call you Dr. Mia Stoll, PhD?" I hear him ask the bride.

"That would be overkill," she says.

"Dr. Mia Stoll then," Uma suggests.

The bride shakes her head. "Too pompous."

Noah cocks his head. "How about just doctor, like in *Doctor Who*?"

The bride grins. "How about just Mia?"

Noah and Uma exchange a comically dubious look and nod in unison. "Yes, doctor."

I join the trio amid peals of laughter.

Noah's smile slips and blood drains from his face the moment he sees me.

"Sophie!" Uma gives me a hug. "So nice to see you here!"

I mumble something. Mia says something and I respond to her. Hopefully, my autopilot is using context-appropriate expressions.

Uma hooks her arm through Mia's and walks away with her.

Noah and I stare at each other.

"Sophie," he says. "I feared this would happen… I tried to call you all day yesterday—"

"I lost my phone."

He swallows. "I went to your place, and I waited, but you didn't come home…"

"Dad took me out, and then I slept over at Mom's."

"That's what I thought." He draws a breath. "Has he… Has he told you about me?"

A sense of foreboding seizes my chest. "What do you mean?"

"I guess he hasn't, then." Noah's lips compress into a hard line. "He just brought you here instead."

My chin begins to tremble.

"I haven't been completely honest with you," Noah says.

I stare at him and, suddenly, I *know*.

All the jagged pieces of the puzzle fall into place, forming a picture that explains everything.

"You're Count d'Arcy's *other* brother," I say.

He nods.

"You're the owner of the estate you took me to last month."

He nods again.

"Why?"

Before he can respond, I lower the pitch of my voice and say mockingly, "I'm Noah Masson, a goalie and a pizza delivery man."

The muscles on his face are so taut they look like they might snap at any moment.

"Why the charade?" I ask.

He grabs my hand. "It wasn't a charade, Sophie. I *am* Noah Masson, goalie and pizza delivery man. That's who I've chosen to be."

"And yet," I smirk. "Your brother is a filthy-rich count and you yourself are worth at least fifteen million."

He says nothing.

"You never even mentioned you had a brother," I say. "Two of them!"

"I didn't mean to—" he begins.

I fake a male voice again. "I'm renting a tiny apartment from you and helping my friend sell his estate. Oh wait, it's *my* estate! My mom volunteers for a charitable foundation. Oh, wait it's *her* foundation. Uma is just a friend. Oh wait, she's actually my *fiancée* with whom I came to my *brother's* wedding."

"She isn't!" Noah almost shouts. "It's not what it looks like."

A few heads turn toward us.

"With you, nothing is what it looks like," I say.

"Sophie, please, can we go somewhere private, so I can explain my reasons… and apologize properly?"

"Don't bother." I yank my hand from his and look around.

Dad is leaning on the wall near an elaborate flower arrangement, watching me anxiously.

I run to him. "Will you take me home?"

He nods, and five minutes later we're in a cab, zooming away to my apartment.

When the mansion vanishes from sight, I wipe my eyes with the back of my hand and turn to Dad. "Will you take me home to Key West?"

TWENTY-THREE
Noah

Oscar gives me a wounded look, followed by a frustrated growl and a long vibrato whimper. That particular sequence means, "Why aren't you sharing that sandwich? I thought we were friends."

"You've put on weight, buddy." I pet him. "The vet says we have to watch your diet."

Oscar whines some more and scampers to the gap between the cupboard and the wall where he stays for a long moment. Coming out, he heads straight to the TV room and climbs on the couch for his midafternoon nap.

I've always wondered what he does in that corner. Maybe it's his meditation room where he performs a breathing routine, reminds himself life isn't so bad, and recovers his mojo. Another possibility is that he keeps a stash of naked lady dog postcards in there to be perused in times of emotional crisis. Whatever happens in that nook clearly works, because he always emerges from it cheered up.

I wish I had a place like that.

Because if this isn't a time of emotional crisis for me, then I don't know what is.

Sophie didn't answer my calls for the next two days following the wedding. When I called from the intercom of her building, she wouldn't buzz me in. Then I left for Athens for a LEN Cup game. The team stayed on for a couple more days to visit the Acropolis and explore the local night life.

Zach and I flew back. I went to Sophie's office straight from the airport. Her colleagues told me my landlady had to cut her internship short and return to the States for personal reasons. A friendly young woman told me *Mademoiselle* Bander had hired the agency to take care of my lease.

"I'm here to help if there's anything you need," she said, giving me her card.

"Thank you, everything's fine."

Heading out the door, I wondered how she'd have reacted if I'd told her the truth, which hasn't changed since July.

I need to kiss Sophie Bander.

So badly that I'm seriously considering going to Key West to try to smooth things over with her. I screwed up, there's no doubt about that. But I did have mitigating circumstances.

Sophie always told me she was going to marry the man of her father's dreams. She had a life plan for her future as a Floridian real estate mogul. She was going back to Key West at Christmastime to start it off. What we had wasn't serious.

Cut the crap, Noah.

These are not "mitigating circumstances." They are cheap, pathetic excuses. The bottom line is, Sophie had been honest and frank with me from start to finish.

And I lied to her.

No wonder she's mad at me.

The problem is I can't go to Key West right now. My team needs me. For the first time since Lucas established the club, we have a serious shot at becoming national champions. We're in the middle of a crazy season, competing in two overlapping championships, *Championnat de France* and the LEN Cup. We train several hours a day, and we travel all the time.

I had to quit my pizza delivery job.

Lucas tells us that now that *Nageurs de Paris* has won enough games to be taken seriously, he has big plans for the club. His first step will be to hire a publicist who will raise sponsor money and get advertising contracts for players.

Let's hope that happens, and soon.

Because I'm running out of funds. The estate hasn't been sold yet. Heck, I haven't even had time to hire an agent. And even when I do, it's not like I intend to keep the proceeds. Assuming Sophie's ballpark is correct, most of the fifteen million will go to Maman's foundation as planned. There will also be a huge tax to pay, and maybe even lawyer fees if Sebastian contests the sale.

Which he might, seeing how much he's attached to preserving the d'Arcy patrimony.

Is that such a bad thing?

I startle at the thought that came out of nowhere. Well, not quite. Ever since Sophie and I went to Burgundy, my mind keeps conjuring up images of the trained vines, of the view on the park from the Salon Bleu, and of Sophie gawking at the down-at-the-heels grandeur of the castle.

"This place is magnificent, for sure, but not just on the outside," she said as we were leaving. "It has a beautiful soul. I hope the new owner can see it and love it the way it deserves to be loved."

My doorbell rings as I swallow the last bite of my sandwich. Oscar wakes up for a split second, then shuts his eyes again, in what I choose to interpret as complete trust in my capacity to handle the intruder.

It must be Maman.

She's taking me to a "lovely" new restaurant she's discovered in my neighborhood, and that's why I just ate a sandwich. Maman's "lovely" restaurants tend to be of the kind that serve beautifully presented itty-bitty portions that never leave me sated.

I let Maman in, glancing at my watch. The reservation is for seven, so I have a full hour to ask her the questions I've been burning to ask since Raphael's wedding.

She heads to the TV room and sits as far from Oscar as she can. She says he's too scruffy. She isn't entirely wrong.

"You invited Mr. Bander to Raphael's wedding just so he'd bring Sophie along and she'd find out the truth about me," I say without a preamble.

She gives me a long stare. "You shouldn't have lied to her."

"You're right, I shouldn't have. And you should've stayed out of it—or advised me to come clean. But, instead, you used my mistake to advance your agenda."

"I had your best interest at heart," she says, "And the same goes for Ludwig who was very concerned that his only daughter would ruin her future."

"By being with me?"

"By abandoning her dreams for an infatuation."

It was more than an infatuation, I burn to say.

Why else would it grow with every passing day and week, instead of fading away? Why else would it feel so right, like I found the woman who was made for me?

But I keep silent, afraid that saying those things out loud will make Sophie's departure even harder to bear.

"By the way," Maman says. "I'm glad your peccadillo led Ludwig to me. What a wonderful, upright man! He believes in charity as much as I do. I'm sure it won't be long before he donates a sizable amount to my foundation."

"No doubt." I squint at her. "So the pair of you came up with a genius fix to the problem Sophie and I created."

"Don't be so cynical," Maman says before simpering. "I must admit, our fix *was* brilliant in its simplicity and effectiveness."

"Just listen to yourself!"

She shrugs. "I did nothing wrong. Sophie is a nice girl, but she's wrong for you."

"Because *you* know who's right for me."

"As it happens, I do." She arches an eyebrow. "Uma."

Of course.

Maman's gaze softens. "She loves you."

"Yes, she does," I say. "As a friend."

"Don't be silly."

"She told me that herself."

Maman blinks, visibly confused. "She couldn't have."

"And yet she did. Maman… I can see how she and I may look like a great match. Only, we aren't drawn to each other."

"You're just saying it to spite me." She rearranges her legs and smoothes her skirt. "You're upset."

Sarcasm contorts my mouth. "No kidding."

"All I wanted was your happiness."

"Did it occur to you to ask if I'd already found my happiness before you walked all over it?"

She blinks again.

Bile rises in my throat. "Tell you what, Maman, you should order some puppets for the foundation and start staging shows."

She shifts uncomfortably. "I'm not sure that's a priority for the children we're helping."

"It won't be just for them—it'll be mostly for you. Your puppets will do *exactly* what you want them to do. And your shows—every single one of them—will end exactly the way you want them to end."

She lifts a trembling hand to her face and rubs her left temple, an expression of suffering on her face.

Migraine.

A.k.a., my cue to apologize and take back everything I've just said, because I've suddenly realized she's right. Because that's how we roll.

But not anymore.

Neither of us speaks for a while.

Then Maman stops rubbing her temple and gazes into my eyes. "I love you, Noah. Please believe me when I say that everything I've done was dictated by that love."

"Oh, I do believe you." I nod for emphasis. "But here's the thing. Your love has soured me. It's poisoned my relationships with Seb and Raph, and now also with Sophie. I'd say something's wrong with your love."

She sniffles and dabs her eyes, which would normally shut me up.

But not this time.

"Your love is broken, Maman," I say. "It needs some serious fixing."

She stands up and storms out the door.

I don't try to stop her.

Instead, my thoughts return to the estate. The more I think of it the less I see how Sophie's enthusiasm about it reflected badly on her. She was just being herself. Candid and genuine. Refreshingly honest. Awestruck by something exceptional—and vocal about it.

Isn't that a thousand times better than hypocrisy?

TWENTY-FOUR
Sophie

Watching the sun dip into the Gulf of Mexico, coloring the sky all shades of purple, reminds me of the view on the park from Noah's castle. I'd announced it was the most beautiful vista in the world, even better than Key West sunsets. I had raved about the chateau and its grounds, and even declared I would do anything to lay my hands on it. Including marrying someone I didn't have deep feelings for.

The shame.

That conversation is, without a doubt, the single most mortifying episode of my life. Just remembering it sets my face on fire. Why, oh why, did I say those things?

I was *making a point.*

And Noah took it.

With a sigh, I scoot from the middle of the bench to the side of the boat, hoping that Doug's friends Tim and Rosalind won't notice my flaming cheeks.

"What do you think, babe?" Doug calls out from behind the helm. "Gorgeous, huh?"

I've lost count of the times I almost asked Doug to call me *bébé*. He probably would as a tribute to my French side. Only there's a risk that hearing him say *bébé* would make things even worse for me. Getting over Noah has been hard enough—I don't need a daily reminder of what he murmured when he made love to me.

It's been only two months, but it seems like my Parisian holiday ended an eternity ago. And yet, it seems like yesterday.

"The sunset or your boat?" I ask Doug, turning my head to give him a bright smile.

Rosalind and Tim chuckle.

"The boat." Doug grins back, proud beyond measure of his shiny new yacht.

"The best view ever!" I say.

Just to think I was a girl who couldn't get the hang of lying no matter how hard she tried.

That girl is gone.

The new me has grown up and figured it out.

Watch me. "Hey, I'm getting a little queasy," I say to Doug, pulling a sad face. "Could you drop me off at the pier?"

He gives me an aww-you-poor-darling look. "Sure thing. Do you mind if we continue without you?"

"Not at all!"

This one isn't a lie. Doug's friends are OK, but we have zero shared interests and nothing to say to each other.

With Doug, at least, I can talk shop.

When I'm finally alone in the house—I've moved back in with Dad until I find a new apartment—I fix myself a cranberry cooler and sit on the porch.

Halfway through my drink, my phone rings in my pocket. It's Noah. I never pick up when he calls me, expecting each call to be the last. But he's been at for eight weeks now, sometimes daily, and there's no sign of him relenting.

Dad says I should just block his number. He's right—that's the best thing to do.

I answer the call.

"Sophie?" he sounds incredulous.

"Yes. I picked up just to ask you to stop calling."

See? I'm so good at lying now it's scary.

What I really picked up for is to hear his voice. And also because it's been so damn hard to stop thinking about him, to forget his eyes, his smile, his lovemaking…

"I'll stop calling if that's what you want," he says. "But will you please hear me out first?"

I huff out a sigh. "It's OK, Noah. I'm not mad anymore. You hid things from me because you had no reason to reveal them. We weren't in a serious relationship."

"Is that what you think?"

"Yes, and I think my dramatic departure from your brother's wedding was utterly ridiculous. I hope you didn't have much explaining to do."

"You've changed," he says.

"Amen to that. What about you? Did you sell the estate?"

"I donated my trust fund to Maman's foundation and kept the estate."

"What will you do with it?"

"Seb and Raph are chipping in with enough to cover the renovations and initial upkeep."

"Seb and Raph, huh? The brothers you hated so much you wouldn't even mention their existence."

There's a brief silence before he says, "I'm done with hate."

Good for you.

"How's the championship looking?" I ask.

"We trounced Bordeaux and Nancy and defeated Marseille, which nobody expected, seeing as they practically own the national championship. Next week, we're headed to Strasbourg for the finals."

"Good luck."

"Thank you, I'll need it." He hesitates. "Not just for the match, but for… everything. The delivery man is now saddled with a huge estate, a crumbling chateau, and a once-profitable winery. I don't even know where to start."

"Hire a manager or bring in an associate."

"I've been thinking about that, too," he says.

"Stop thinking—act."

He chuckles.

"It was nice talking—" I begin.

"Would *you* like to be my associate and spearhead all of the cool projects you came up with in Burgundy?"

Whoa.

"Thank you for offering," I say, "But I'm going to say no."

"Sophie, I—"

This time it's my turn to cut in. "I'm about to get a marriage proposal."

"From whom?"

"A lovely local man—our biggest competitor, as it happens. Well, ex-competitor now."

"Has your ex-competitor penciled a date onto your calendar?" he asks with sarcasm.

"In fact, he has. Next Saturday at Louie's Backyard."

Why I'm giving him the time and place, I do not know. It's not like he's going to fly in from France and *save* me.

Anyway, I don't *need* saving.

There's a pause before Noah speaks. "I take it you intend to say yes."

"You bet."

I do intend to say yes, despite my panic attacks in the middle of the night, doubts, and the knowledge I'll never feel about Doug the way I feel... *felt* about Noah.

"Isn't it too soon for a proposal?" he asks. "You couldn't have dated him more than two months."

"Why wait? Doug and I are a great match, personally and professionally."

Except, my body still refuses to allow him more than a no-tongues smooch every now and then.

It's back to frigid for me.

Doug says he doesn't mind. He claims that my *decorum* is one of the things he likes about me. I never gave him the reason why I left Paris earlier than planned, but he's come up with an explanation of his own. That city was too decadent for Sophie Bander. Doug is extremely proud to be dating the most uptight woman in Key West.

The image of Noah's blond head between my widespread thighs with my fingers delving into his soft hair as I guide him flashes before my eyes.

It's hard to believe that woman was me.

But what happens in Paris, stays in Paris.

"You told me once," Noah says, "that you avoided emotions because they cloud your judgment."

"So?"

"Can't you see that's what's happening to you now? You're letting an emotion cloud your judgment. And it isn't even a good emotion."

"What are you talking about?"

"Anger."

I say nothing.

"You are still mad at me," he says. "And you want to hurt me as much as I hurt you."

"It's not about you! I'm over you. I'll marry Doug because he's the kind of man I've always wanted to end up with."

"Listen to me, *bébé*. Don't repeat my mistakes. I let anger guide me for years, but things weren't as black and white as I thought. The villains had redeeming qualities, and the saint… wasn't so saintly."

"So you turned your back on Marguerite?"

"Of course not. I still love her, and I admire her commitment to philanthropy. But I'm no longer the tool of her revenge."

"I'm glad to hear it," I say.

"*Bébé*—"

"Take good care, Noah."

And with that, I hang up.

TWENTY-FIVE
Noah

The first thing I see as I get off the plane is a big sign on the passenger terminal: WELCOME TO THE CONCH REPUBLIC.

I smile.

Sophie told me how Key West jokingly "seceded" from the United States in protest for something back in the eighties. I knew the locals enjoyed their fake independence, but I didn't quite expect a sign at the airport.

Another surprise is that it isn't as hot as I was bracing myself for. But it *is* mid-December.

It's almost *winter*.

After I pass through customs, I head to the taxi line. The hotel I'm booked at is out of town and pricey, but that's what you get when you reserve last minute. And let's not even talk about my business-class airfare; it's the most I've ever paid for a ticket. Actually, for anything. I emptied my savings account and I'm overdrawn, but I didn't touch the estate renovation account that Seb and Raph set up.

It had felt wrong.

Climbing into the cab, I give the driver the address. Amusement flickers in his eyes, but he just drops my duffle into the trunk and drives off.

Exactly one minute later, the cabbie pulls into the front yard of a large wooden mansion with a sign that says, "Marnie's Bed and Breakfast."

It would've taken me five minutes to walk here.

"Twenty dollars," the driver says, pointing to the price list taped to the outside of the car.

I pay, grab my duffel, and head for the entrance of the bed-and-breakfast. In my peripheral vision, I spot something unusual a couple of meters to my left. It's a toy iguana that someone has placed under the palm tree.

Must be the local version of the garden gnome.

The iguana tilts its little head and scurries up the trunk of the tree.

Noah, you're not in Paris anymore.

By the time I've checked in, showered, changed into a fresh set of clothes and returned to the lobby, it's already dark.

"How far are we from Louie's Backyard?" I ask the guy at the front desk.

"A twenty-minute drive. Twenty-five, tops."

"Can you call me a cab?"

"I just tried for another customer," he says, "but the wait is about thirty minutes right now. There's the Poultry Farmers' Convention—"

"Never mind. I'll walk there."

"It's too far for a walk," the concierge says. "You could rent one of our bikes."

I could—and I do.

Any chunk of time gained at this point, even if it's just a five-minute nugget, may change my life.

The concierge gives me directions, hands me a helmet and a lock, and sends me on my way.

It's not until I'm riding in the dark along a narrow strip between the ocean and the highway, my eyes veiled by wind and rain, that I admit I should've walked.

The bike isn't the problem—it's me.

I'm the weak link, wasted from two consecutive flights and too little food. The receptionist said it was easy-peasy. "Just ride along the water past the AIDS Memorial, Higgs Beach, and Casa Marina until you see Louie's Backyard."

Maybe, instead of trusting him, I should've asked for a map or, at least, for a description of the AIDS Memorial. As it is, I'm riding blind, separated from the ocean on my left by a low guardrail and from the highway on my right by nothing. I have no clue where I am.

Suddenly, my front wheel meets an obstacle, and I fly off the bike and over the guardrail.

Fuck!

At least, I won't drown, I tell myself as I fall.

Thump! Splash!

I don't, but it isn't thanks to my swimming skills.

It's because my bum hits the sandy bottom of the ocean, and I topple over on my side.

The water is so shallow it barely covers me, even lying down.

I lever myself up to a sitting position and laugh, feeling both relieved and ridiculous for expecting a serious plunge.

When I push open the door of Louie's Backyard, I'm soaked to my bones and sore in several places. Did I mention it's nine?

I spot Sophie at a table by the window, with a well-groomed man in his early thirties. There are two empty dessert plates on the table, a check folder, and some change.

Fuck.

He must've proposed by now.

"Hi," I say to both before training my gaze on Sophie. "Can we talk?"

"Noah!" She moves to stand up but then sinks back into her chair.

The man surveys me.

I stare at Sophie. Water drips from my hair and clothes, forming a puddle on the floor. All I can think of is whether I am too late or if there's still time to talk Sophie out of marrying this guy.

He turns to her. "Who is this?"

"Someone I met in Paris," she says, looking shaken.

He searches her face. "Should I *ask* him to leave?"

There's a clear implication of potential violence in his tone, should I unwisely decline his request.

Dude, I may be drenched, but I'm still bigger than you.

My gaze is locked on Sophie's mouth. Boy, how I've missed it!

I hope she says "don't" to her beau. I pray she doesn't say "get out!" to me.

Sophie gives him a weak smile. "I'm sorry, Doug. There's some unfinished business Noah and I need to discuss."

She stands up.

Doug stands too. "Are you sure?"

She nods.

"Call me if he tries anything funny," he says.

"I will." She marches toward the exit.

I follow her. Once outside, she continues to walk briskly. I settle into a stride next to her. Ten minutes later, we're on an empty beach.

Sitting down, she hugs her knees and looks up at me.

I slump to the sand by her side.

"Talk," she says with her gaze on the water.

"Did you say yes to Doug?"

She keeps looking straight ahead. "What if I did?"

Fuck.

I drop my head into my hands.

"I said no," she breathes out.

I turn to her.

She's looking at me now, and even in the dark, I can see the turmoil she's going through in her eyes.

"I'm stupid," she says. "Doug is really a perfect catch."

"Then why did you say no?"

"I can't imagine… making love to him."

On impulse, I grab her hand. "I love you, Sophie."

She blinks. "What about your amazing Uma?"

"She's still amazing and will always be." I lift her hand to my lips. "But she has no effect on the pace of my heart or on the stiffness of my cock."

I press my lips to the back of her hand, remembering her skin. *Ooh, the bliss.* Flipping her hand over, I kiss the inside of her palm, her wrist, her fingers.

"Shouldn't you be in Strasbourg now?" she asks.

"I should—and yet I'm here."

She frowns. "But it's the finals, the chance to win that gold you've been dreaming about—"

"We have a substitute for each player, including me. No big deal."

The crease between her eyebrows deepens.

I exhale a long breath. "OK, here's the truth. They might lose. If they do, they'll hate me. Actually, they hate me already. I hate myself for walking out on them like this."

"You shouldn't have!"

I stare into her expressive eyes. "I have no regrets, Sophie. If you're willing to give me another chance, I'll quit everything and move here."

Her eyes widen. "You would?"

"In a heartbeat."

She tilts her head to the side, her expression still concerned.

"Maybe I can find a water polo club to join here," I say, winking. "Or a pizza joint in need of delivery men."

She draws closer and peers into my eyes. "You'd really do that for a second chance with me?"

I nod.

Her lips part slightly.

I lean in and claim them. Soft, full, warm. Holding her face, I sweep my tongue over her lips. She parts them, letting me in. *Sweet Jesus, that taste!* I drink it in, pushing my tongue deeper. Can't get enough of her. Fifty-seven days of craving this, of starving for her, of waking up with a hard-on, furious for being torn out of the dream where I could hold her.

I'm never going without Sophie that long again.

Ever.

When we break the kiss to catch our breaths, she leans her forehead against mine and murmurs, "I'll go to France with you."

I draw back and study her face, incredulous.

She smiles.

"Are you sure?" I ask.

She nods. "I love you."

I gather her to me and kiss her again, hungrily, thoroughly.

A few moments later, she draws back. There's a mixture of surprise and elation in her beautiful eyes as she guides my hand under the hem of her dress.

I gloss my fingertips up her inner thigh until they meet the material of her panties. It's moist. I apply more pressure, sliding my fingers a little farther.

The fabric isn't just moist—it's sopping wet.

If we weren't on a public beach, I'd unzip my jeans, sit her astride my lap, and drive into her like a madman.

"*Bébé*," I murmur, slipping a finger under the panties and into her hot slickness.

Her eyes roll in her head.

When she focuses on my face again, her expression is unexpectedly determined. "We need a room."

"Will my hotel do?" I withdraw my finger.

"Yeah." She reaches for her purse and stands. "Let's go."

I remain seated, waiting for my arousal to die down.

It takes time, what with Sophie's eagerness messing with my willpower.

But that's OK, because the urgency in her voice is a gratification in its own right. As for the hunger in her eyes, it's worth the championship gold I forfeited by coming here.

It's worth all the gold in the world.

TWENTY-SIX
Sophie

When we enter Noah's room after a half-hour power hike, both of us need a shower.

So we take it together with a condom for company.

As soon as we've washed the sweat and sand off each other, Noah puts the condom on and backs me against the tiled wall. I moan from the joy of having his body pressed to mine. He kisses me gently, then harder, and then applies himself to getting me to the point of arousal I was at on the beach.

It doesn't take long.

Truth is, I think I could get there just by looking at his wet muscled chest or peering into his blue eyes I could drown in—have drowned in.

I'm beyond salvation.

He murmurs my name as he fondles my breasts and sucks my stiff nipples. His hands roam my body, rubbing, gripping, squeezing.

When he bends his knees to hoist me high against him, I throw my arms around his neck and bracket his waist with my legs. My body tenses with need as he devours my mouth. All I can think of is the thickness at my opening and how much I want it. My core is heavy, aching, pulling, begging for the feel of it.

I'm ready.

So ready I'm on the verge of exploding.

And that's exactly what I do, seconds after he buries himself in me hilt-deep.

The orgasm is shockingly, achingly sweet. It pushes everything else outside of the confines of my world. It connects my core with my mind in a profound, almost supernatural way, stealing my breath.

When it ebbs, leaving me both sated and hungry for more, I realize I've just experienced pleasure like nothing I've ever known before.

I want this again—I *need* this again—as many times and as often as Noah can handle.

"Did you just…?" he asks, not daring to utter the word.

I nod.

"Good girl." His face expands into a smug grin.

I grin back. "Wouldn't mind another one."

He stops smiling and slams into me. This thrust is sharp and rough, unlike the long stroke he used to enter me, but it's so exquisitely erotic I gasp.

He begins to hammer, and all I can do is grip his neck and cling to him, letting the pleasure build inside me. My fingers dig into his flesh as he pounds, fierce, abandoning himself to his own need. Our bodies strain together, muscles taut, blood rushing, hearts throbbing.

With every withdrawal, I feel emptier than before. With every push, I'm propelled closer to another climax.

When it ripples through me, making me cry out, Noah growls and lets himself come, too. Our voices mingle as our bodies quake with pleasure.

Afterward, we towel each other off and climb into the bed.

"Another one?" he asks, looking keen and awfully pleased with himself.

"Enough for tonight, I'm wasted."

He cups my cheek. "Tomorrow morning, then."

"First thing," I promise.

He strokes my face, when I notice a small crease between his eyebrows. "Something wrong?"

"Your life plan." He frowns. "What about your dream of becoming your dad's associate and the biggest realtor in Florida?"

I touch the hollow above his collarbone and rest my hand on his strong neck. "Every good plan allows for adjustments. I'll launch my conquest of the world from Paris."

He stares into my eyes for a long moment. "How about launching it from Burgundy?"

"Are you asking me to run the estate so you can keep playing pro water polo?"

"Yes."

"I'd love to," I say, "but that would make you my boss, which would be—"

He presses a finger against my lips, shushing me. "I'm not asking you to run *my* estate as a manager. I'm asking if you'd do me the honor of running *our* estate, as my wife."

EPILOGUE
Sophie

I look around the great hall of the Chateau d'Arcy, filled with music, light and people—just the way it was built to be—and grin, satisfied.

It's been an eventful couple of months for Noah and me.

Zach had surpassed himself in Strasbourg, scoring like a madman. Not just Zach—every single player did his darnedest to help the club snag the gold medal. Problem was, they couldn't be as focused on offense as in the previous games because the substitute goalie needed more help than Noah to block the opponent's incessant attacks.

Strasbourg had won gold for three years straight for a reason.

At the end of the last quarter the score was tied, and the referee announced a penalty shootout.

Under normal circumstances, that would've been a perfect opportunity for Noah's perfect saves. But he happened to be across the ocean at that moment, trying to make an entirely different kind of catch.

His club lost.

Back in Paris, *Nageurs* was still celebrated for the silver—a first for the city—but all the players could think of was how close they'd been to the gold.

Strasbourg's coach retired in late January, just as he'd been planning to, and Lucas succeeded him as head coach for the national team.

The day after we landed at Charles de Gaulle, Noah showed up for the workout at the pool. He was fully prepared to be roasted by Lucas and his teammates and kicked out of the club.

He did get roasted, but in the end, Lucas chose to give him a second chance.

"If you pull another stunt like that on me," Coach said, "you're dead."

Noah swore he wouldn't.

Seeing as he had absolutely no intention of proposing again.

Seeing as his first proposal got accepted.

And that brings me to the reason why the great hall is bustling with smartly dressed people on this frosty late-February evening.

Noah and I are celebrating our engagement.

Everyone's here.

My mom, looking young and flirty in her shimmery red dress.

My dad, tall and fit and all Denzel-y.

Marguerite, making eyes at him.

A bunch of philanthropists and high-level officials Marguerite has invited so she can tell them about the foundation.

Noah's brothers Raphael and Sebastian, their wives Mia and Diane, babies Lily and Tanguy, and some of their in-laws.

Sue and two other friends of mine from back home.

Uma, dazzling in a gold and silver embroidered sari.

Jacqueline and the rest of the estate staff.

Noah's entire team with their plus-ones.

The Derzians.

Oscar.

Jazzy music is playing in the background, and several couples are dancing.

Noah is talking with his brothers whom he's been spending a lot of time with lately. Raphael says something funny or—judging by the mischievous expression on his face—naughty, and both Noah and Sebastian burst out laughing. It's incredible how thick the three of them have grown over just a few months. Of course, the two older brothers had been close from the start, but Noah had barely spoken to either of them since Marguerite whisked him off to Nepal when he was eight.

I guess blood *is* thicker than water.

Their blossoming bromance aside, the trio is easy on the eyes, with Noah being the tallest, brawniest, and blondest of the lot.

I really should stop ogling my fiancé like that—there'll be plenty of time for it when the guests are gone.

With an effort, I peel my eyes away from him and look for Diane's sister, Chloe, who's an architect and property flipper. I want to consult with her about the renovations we're planning in the spring.

As I scan the crowd for a petite woman who meets her description, I catch sight of Marguerite sashaying toward Dad.

"Ludwig!" She touches his arm. "Finally, we can catch up."

"How have you been?" he asks politely.

When I'd learned about Dad's involvement in what Noah and I now refer to as the "Parents to the Rescue Conspiracy," I cold-shouldered him for a week.

Then I forgave him.

He's my dad.

I know he sent a fat check to Nepal last month, and Marguerite wrote back that she'd like to show him how grateful she was, when they met in person.

Ugh.

"I've been busy," she says, "but also thrilled to launch all those new health, housing, and literacy programs with the money that came in over the last few months."

"I'm happy to hear that."

"Now, Ludwig," she says in a husky voice. "About that promise I made in my letter—"

"Ah, there she is," Dad interrupts her, waving to Mom. "Cat, over here!"

When she's close enough, he grabs her hand and pulls her to him.

"*Comment ça va,* Marguerite?" Mom asks with a tight smile.

The other French woman's smile is just as cursory. "*Très bien,* Catherine."

"Cat is my girlfriend," Dad says to Marguerite.

Oh. My. God.

I knew he'd taken Mom to dinner a few times, but him calling her his *girlfriend* means that the rekindled relationship has progressed to a whole new level.

A mischievous smile dances in Dad's eyes.

Oh, how I love that smile.

Marguerite turns to Mom. "I thought you were divorced."

"We are," Mom says.

Dad lifts her hand to his lips. "I hope we'll put an end to that unfortunate situation soon."

What?

I freeze.

Mom gasps.

"Am I a fool to hope for that?" Dad asks her.

She narrows her eyes at him. "Are you asking what I think you're asking?"

He nods.

She screws up her face. "What if we botch it again?"

"We won't," he says. "I promise. And just so you believe me, I'm no longer the manager of my agency. My new associate Doug Thompson will take care of the day-to-day business so I can spend at least half the year in France with my two beauties."

This is too good to be true.

Mom's face expands into a beaming grin. "Then it's an *oui*."

"Congratulations," Marguerite mutters and retreats hurriedly.

"Whee!" someone squeaks in delight, clapping her hands.

It may or may not be me.

I dart to them and pull both into a big hug.

"Guys," I say. "You just made my most cherished dream come true."

Mom and Dad gaze at each other, eyes glistening.

I smooch each of them on the cheek. "Will you lovebirds excuse me for a moment? I need to share this scoop with my *fiancé*."

As I make my way to Noah, who's now discussing something with Zach, he turns to me and looks into my eyes.

A little miracle happens.

Despite all the laws of physics—quantum or otherwise—despite the distance between us, I feel him touch me in the deepest, most intimate way.

Soul to naked soul.

Author's Note

Water Polo

One of the earliest Olympic sports, water polo is a national pastime in Hungary, Serbia and Montenegro, and is very popular in most of Europe. But it's incomprehensibly underfunded in other parts of the world, including France and the United States. Things are changing in the US, though, where water polo is the fastest growing sport. No wonder, considering the achievements of the national men's team (Olympic silver at Beijing) and, especially, women's team (Olympic gold at both London and Rio).

For the purposes of this story, I invented several water polo clubs, tweaked the schedules of various competitions, and threw in a fake fact or two, such as Paris winning a silver medal in the national championship.

But I've tried to stick as close to reality as possible.

Chateau d'Arcy

The Chateau d'Arcy in this book is fictional. It was inspired by several castles I've visited in the Loire Valley, Normandy and Burgundy. A real Chateau d'Arcy exists, located near the village of Chaumes-en-Brie in Burgundy. Previously home to viscounts and barons, it is now the property of the French State.

The Grotte d'Arcy is real, and it does have amazing Ice Age rock art. Totally worth a visit.

Bonus Content

FREE BOOK!

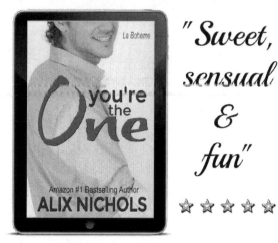

"*Sweet, sensual & fun*"

Get a **free novella** in the La Bohème
series: **bit.ly/alix-freebook**

~ ~ ~

Book Chapters

Find You in Paris
(The Darcy Brothers)

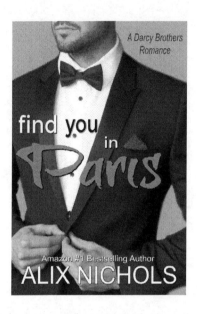

If there's one man that store clerk and amateur photographer Diane Petit really, really, actively hates, it's fragrance mogul Sebastian Darcy who stole her father's company--and wrecked the man's health in the process.
But the arrogant SOB had better brace himself because Diane has vowed revenge.
And revenge she will have.

~ ~ ~

Chapter One

It is a truth universally acknowledged that a young man in possession of a vast fortune must be an entitled SOB born into money. Either that or a rags-to-riches a-hole who bulldozed his way to said fortune, leaving maimed bodies in his wake.

The ferocious-looking PA returns to her desk. "Monsieur Darcy is still in a meeting."

"That's OK." I smile benignly. "I can wait."

I place my hands demurely on my knees and stare at the portrait adorning—or should I say disfiguring—the wall across the hallway from where I'm seated.

Pictured is Count Sebastian d'Arcy du Grand-Thouars de Saint-Maurice, the oldest son of the late Count Thibaud d'Arcy du Grand-Thouars de Saint-Maurice and the inheritor of an estate estimated at around one billion euros. Said estate isn't your run-of-the-mill stock holdings or start-up fortune. Oh no. It's made up of possessions that were handed down—uninterrupted and snowballing—all the way from the Middle Ages.

Even Robespierre and his fellow revolutionaries didn't get their greedy little hands on the d'Arcy fortune.

What are the odds?

Upon his father's premature demise ten years ago, young Sebastian moved back into the town house in the heart of Le Marais and took the reins of the family's main business. A twenty-three-year-old greenhorn at the time, you'd expect him to make tons of bad decisions and sink the company or, at least, diminish its value.

But no such luck.

Instead, Sebastian Darcy took Parfums d'Arcy from number three to the number one European flavor and fragrance producer — a feat that neither his illustrious grandfather nor his star-crossed father had managed to accomplish.

According to my research, also about ten years ago, the new count chose to go by "Darcy," abandoning the apostrophe and the rest of his status-laden name. I'm sure he only did it to fool those *beneath* him — which includes most everyone in a country that guillotined its royals — into believing that he sees himself as their equal.

The hell he does.

Sebastian Darcy is a stinking-rich aristocrat with instincts of an unscrupulous business shark. This means he qualifies in both the SOB and the a-hole categories.

No, scratch that. He *slays* both categories.

And I hate him more than words can say.

The straitlaced man on the wall seems to smirk. I shudder, my nerves taut to the point of snapping. Will they kick me out if I spit at the photo? Of course they will. I steal a glance at the PA stationed between me and Darcy's office. She looks like a cross between a human and a pit bull. I'm sure she'd love to stick something other than paper between the jaws of her sturdy hole punch.

My hand, for example.

But I didn't come here to fight with Darcy's PA. I'll keep my saliva in my mouth, my eyes cast down, my butt perched on the edge of the designer chair, and my knees drawn together and folded to the side.

Like the meek little mouse I'm trying to pass for.

After waiting three weeks, I'm careful not to arouse any suspicion in Pitbull's mind so she won't cancel my appointment with Darcy.

Eyes on the prize, Diane! Don't forget you're here to declare war by spitting in Count Sebastian Darcy's face, rather than at his photographic representation.

I look at the photo again, arranged in perfect symmetry between the portraits of his grandfather, Bernard, who founded the company, and his father, Thibaud, who almost put the lid on it. I know this because I've done my homework.

During my week-long research, I dug up every piece of information the Internet had to offer about Sebastian Darcy and his family. I was hoping to find dirt, and I did. The only problem was it was already out in the open—common knowledge, yesterday's news.

And completely useless as leverage.

Pitbull looks up from her smartphone. "Monsieur Darcy is delayed. Do you mind waiting a little longer?"

"No problem." I smile politely. "I'm free this afternoon."

She arches an eyebrow as if having a free afternoon is something reprehensible.

How I wish I could stick out my tongue! But instead I widen my already unnaturally wide smile.

She frowns, clearly not buying it.

I turn away and stare at Darcy's likeness again. In addition to the now-stale scandal, my research has revealed that Darcy is close to his middle brother, Raphael, and also to a longtime friend—Laurent something or other. Our vulture-man even managed to have a serious girlfriend for most of last year. A food-chain heiress, she looked smashing at the various soirées, galas, and fundraisers where she was photographed on his arm. Darcy was rumored to be so into his rich beauty he was about to propose. But then she suddenly dumped him about six months ago.

Clever girl.

He has no right to be happy when Dad's life is in shambles.

I won't stop until I crush him, even if it means I go to jail—or to hell—for using black-hat tactics. It's not as if they'd let me into heaven, anyway. I've already broken the arms and legs on Darcy's voodoo doll.

There's no turning back after you do that sort of thing.

The next step is to let the world know who he really is and hurt him in a variety of ways, big and small. And then, just before delivering the deathblow, let him know he's paying for his sins.

That's why my first move is to show him my face and make sure he remembers it and associates it with *unpleasantness*. That way, when the shit hits the fan, he'll know which creditor is collecting her debt.

Pitbull breaks me out of my dream world. "Monsieur Darcy's meeting is running late."

"That's OK, I can—"

"No," she cuts me off. "There's no point in waiting anymore. As soon as the meeting is over, he'll head to the 9th arrondissement, where he's expected at a private reception."

I stand up.

She glances at my bare ring finger. "Mademoiselle, I can reschedule you for Friday, December twelfth. It's two months away, but that's the only—"

"Thank you, but that won't be necessary," I say.

I know exactly which reception Sebastian Darcy is going to tonight.

Chapter Two

Three months later

"It might snow tonight." Octave holds my coat while I wrap a scarf around my neck. "Will monsieur be taking his supper at home?"

As always, I wince at "monsieur," but I do my best not to show it.

Grandpapa Bernard hired Octave before I was born. Roughly Papa's age and a bear of a man, Octave has worked for my family for thirty-odd years, rising from valet to *majordome*. He's seen Raphael, Noah, and me in all kinds of embarrassing situations young boys tend to get themselves into. I've asked him a thousand times to call me Sebastian.

All in vain.

Octave Rossi claims his respect for my *old* family name, my *noble* title, and my position in society is too strong for him to drop the "monsieur."

So be it.

"Yes," I say. "But I'll come home late, so please tell Lynette to make something light. And don't stay up for me."

He nods. "*Oui*, monsieur."

Chances are he'll be up until I get home.

Since I moved back into the town house after Papa's passing, Octave has been helpful in a way no one, not even Maman—especially not Maman—has ever been. All the little things, from paying electricity bills and hiring help to undertaking necessary repairs and planning reception menus, are taken care of with remarkable efficiency.

When he offered to assist me with my correspondence, I insisted on doubling his salary. My argument was that he'd be saving me the expense of a second PA for private matters.

He caved in only after I threatened to move out and sell the house.

I trust him more than anyone.

"Morning, Sebastian! To the office?" my chauffeur, Greg, asks.

He, at least, doesn't have a problem calling me by my first name.

"We'll make a detour," I say as I climb into the Toyota Prius. "I need to see someone first."

I give him the address, and he drives me to the Franprix on rue de la Chapelle in the 18th arrondissement. Greg parks the car, and I march into the supermarket, scanning the cashiers' counters lined parallel to the shop windows.

There she is!

Diane Petit smiles at a customer as she hands her a bag of groceries. She'll be finishing her shift in about ten minutes, according to the private eye I hired to locate and tail her. I'll talk to her then.

Right now, I pretend to study the selection of batteries and gift cards on display not far from her desk. What I'm really doing is furtively surveying the firebrand who smashed a cream cake in my face in front of a few dozen people last October. At the time, the only thing I registered about her through my surprise and anger was *foxy*

I've had ample opportunity to pour over her pretty face and eye-pleasing shape in the numerous close-ups the PI has supplied over the past few weeks. I've studied Diane in all kinds of situations and circumstances—at work with her customers, hanging out with her friends, and roaming the streets with her camera, immortalizing everyday scenes of Parisian life. She's hot, all right, but there's also something endearing about her, something unsophisticated and very un-Parisian.

In spite of her extravagant outburst at Jeanne's bash, Diane Petit seems to be an unpretentious small-town bumpkin through and through.

I've learned a good deal about her since that memorable evening. I know she works part time at this supermarket, lives in a high-rise in the 14th, and hangs out with her foster sister Chloe, a coworker named Elorie, and a waitress named Manon.

She enjoys photographing random things, going to the movies, eating chocolate, and drinking cappuccino.

More importantly, I know why Diane did what she did that night at *La Bohème*.

And I plan to use it to my advantage.

Someone gives me a sharp prod in the back.

"Why are you here?" Diane asks as I spin around.

"To give you a chance to apologize."

She smirks. "You're wasting your time."

"No apology, then?"

"You're here to let me know you're on to me, right?" She puffs out her chest. "Read my lips — I'm not afraid of you."

"That's not why I'm here."

"How did you find me, anyway?"

"I hired a professional who tracked you down within days."

She tilts her head to the side. "And you've waited three months before confronting me. Why?"

"I wanted to know what your deal was, so I gave my PI the time to compile a solid profile." I hesitate before adding, "Besides, your foster sister was shot, and you were busy looking after her. I wanted to wait until Chloe had fully recovered."

"You've met Chloe?" She sounds surprised.

"Of course." I shrug. "Jeanne introduced us."

She blows out her cheeks. "What do you want, Darcy?"

"Just to talk."

"About what?"

"I have a proposition that might interest you."

She looks me over. "Unless your proposition is to give me a magic wand that would turn you into a piglet, I'm not interested."

"I obviously can't do that, but what I can do is —"

"Hey, Elorie, are we still on?" Diane calls to a fellow cashier who passes by.

Elorie smiles. "Only if you and Manon let me choose the movie."

"Fine with me, but I can't vouch for Manon."

While Diane and Elorie discuss the time and place of their outing, I resolve to draw Diane somewhere else before making my offer. Preferably, somewhere that's on my turf rather than hers.

"Can we go someplace quieter?" I ask Diane after Elorie leaves.

She sighs. "OK, but don't take it as a good sign."

"Understood."

I do take it as a step in the right direction, though.

She follows me outside and into the car.

"To Le Big Ben, please," I say to Greg.

He nods, and thirty minutes later, Diane and I are seated in a private booth at my favorite Parisian gentlemen's club, which I also happen to co-own with Raphael as of three weeks ago. We've kept the old manager, who's doing an admirable job. I've continued coming here with Laurent or Raph, as a longtime patron who enjoys the subdued elegance of this place and its unparalleled selection of whiskeys. The staff may not even realize the club has changed hands. It's easier this way—and it removes the need for socializing with them.

"So," Diane says after the server brings my espresso and her cappuccino. "What's your proposition?"

"Marry me."

She blinks and bursts out laughing as if I just said something outrageous. Which I guess it was without prior explanation.

Maybe I should start over.

"Here's the deal," I say. "You and I will *date* through April." I make air quotes when I say "date."

She looks at me as if I've lost my mind.

"You'll *move in* with me in May," I continue. "About a month after that, we'll get *married*."

Diane makes a circular motion with her index at the side of her head and mouths, "Nutcase."

"A month into our marriage, I'll *cheat* on you," I continue, undeterred, with a quote unquote on *cheat*. "And then you'll *leave* me."

She gives me a long stare. "Why?"

"It doesn't concern you. What you need to know is that I'm prepared to pay fifty thousand euros for a maximum of six months in a pretend relationship."

"Why?" she asks again.

"You don't need to know that."

"OK, let me ask you something I do need to know." She arches an eyebrow. "Why *me*?"

I shrug.

"If you continue ignoring my legitimate questions," she says, "I'm out of here before you finish your espresso."

"You're perfect for a plan I'd like to set in motion," I say. "And as an incentive for you to play your role the best you can, I'll quadruple your fee if my plan succeeds."

"How will I know if it succeeds if you won't even tell me what it is?"

"Trust me, you'll know." I smirk. "Everyone in my entourage will."

Diane leans back with her arms crossed over her chest. "Can't you find another candidate for your shady scheme? It couldn't have escaped your notice that I humiliated you in public."

"I assure you it didn't," I say. "But what's really important and valuable here is that it didn't escape other people's notice, either. A picture of my cream-cake-covered mug even ended up in a tabloid or two."

She gives me a smug smile.

"At the time, I told everyone I didn't know you, but I can easily change my tune and *confess* we'd been dating."

"This doesn't make any sense."

"Believe me, it does — a whole lot of sense — if you consider it in light of my scheme."

"Which I can't do," she cuts in, "because you won't tell me what your scheme is."

True. "Anyway, I'll tell everyone we've talked it over and made up."

She says nothing.

"Mademoiselle Petit… Diane." I lean in. "Your parents — and yourself — are *not* in the best financial shape right now. I'm offering an easy solution to your woes."

"Ha!" she interjects with an angry gleam in her almond-shaped eyes. "Says the person who caused our woes!"

She's right, of course, but not entirely. Before going in for the kill, I did offer to buy out her father's fragrance company. The offer wasn't generous by any measure, but it was reasonable given the circumstances. Charles Petit's artisanal workshop wasn't doing terribly well. In fact, it was of little interest to me, with the exception of the two or three of his signature fragrances that were worth the price I'd offered. Charles is a lousy businessman—but he's a true artist. He *created* the fragrances he sold, and he also created for others. I would've offered him a job in one of my labs had I not been one hundred percent sure he'd decline it.

As it happened, he also declined my fifty thousand, calling me a scumbag and a few other choice epithets I won't repeat in front of a lady. Fifty thousand euros isn't a fortune, but seeing as he stood no chance against me, he should've taken the money.

It was better than nothing.

But Charles Petit proved to be more emotional than rational about his business. And he ended up with nothing. Worse than nothing, actually. I heard he took to drinking, got kicked out by his wife, and had a heart attack. Or was it a stroke?

Anyway, my point is, at least some of those misfortunes could've been avoided had he sold his company to me.

I open my mouth to say this to Diane, but then it occurs to me she must already know about my offer. She probably also shares Monsieur Petit's opinion that it was indecently low.

"Can we skip the whole dating and marrying nonsense," Diane says, "and go straight to the part where you grovel at my dad's feet, thrust a check for two hundred thousand into his hand, and beg him to take it in the hopes he might forgive you one day?"

I sigh and shake my head.

She stands. "The answer is no."

"Why don't you think it over? I'll be in touch next week." I set a twenty on the table. "May I offer you a ride?"

"Thank you, Monsieur Darcy, you're very *kind*." She bares her teeth in a smile that doesn't even try to pass for a real one. "But I prefer the *métro*."

End of Chapter

Amanda's Guide to Love
(La Bohème Series)

Parisian career woman Amanda Roussel lives in denial of her desperate loneliness.

Gypsy gambler Kes Moreno knows he's in trouble when he falls for Amanda after a one-night stand.

Can he convince the snarky belle they're right for each other?

~ ~ ~

Chapter One
Rock Bottom

A Woman's Guide to Perfection
Guideline # 1
The Perfect Woman doesn't do one-night stands.

Rationale: One-night stands (ONS) are always disappointing, often hazardous, and invariably awkward.

A word of caution: If you are a frequent ONSer, shut this book right now and give it to someone who may benefit from it. You will never be a Perfect Woman. *Ever*.

Permissible exception: A prolonged dry spell between boyfriends or a highly stressful life event.

Damage control: (a) make sure the sex is safe, (b) make sure your person is safe, (c) leave or kick him or her out before breakfast, (d) wash your body squeaky clean, (e) scrub the memory of the episode from your brain.

Pitfalls to avoid: (a) giving him or her your phone number, (b) telling your best friend about it, (c) thinking that a one-night stand could ever lead to a relationship.

~ ~ ~

Amanda stared at the typed letter. Neatly strung words zoomed in and out of focus as their meaning sank in. *Mademoiselle Roussel . . . I regret to inform you . . . with immediate effect.*

She swallowed hard and slipped the letter into her purse.

Most of her colleagues would cheer at the news. They'd rush into each other's offices and say, "Did you hear? Viper Tongue got the sack! Serves her right." Some of them might send around an e-mail invite for a celebratory drink. Others would just shrug and say good riddance.

Would anyone feel sorry for her? She furrowed her brow. Karine would. And maybe Paul from accounting. Perhaps even Sylvie from marketing, unless she was on meds again and not feeling anything at all.

But none of it really mattered.

What did matter was that the end of the world was upon her. Her personal, localized Armageddon had arrived in an innocent-looking envelope with the Energie NordSud logo on it.

Amanda grabbed her handbag and marched out the door. Keeping her back as straight as she could, she strode through the hallway, down the marble staircase, and out the main entrance.

Eyes on the gate, one foot in front of the other.

She nodded to the security guard and passed through the turnstile.

"Mademoiselle Roussel?" the guard asked, looking at his computer screen and then at her.

"Yes?"

"I must collect your access card."

"I'll come back next week to gather my things," she said as flatly as she could, handing him her card.

He nodded. "We'll let you in. Just make sure your visit is supervised by Monsieur Barre."

"Of course."

Amanda turned on her heel and marched away, hoping the guard hadn't seen her grimace. Truth was she'd rather donate her fine glass paperweight and Bodum French press to the company than ask Julien Barre—the bastard who'd fired her—to allow her to clean out her desk.

And have him breathe down her neck while she was doing it.

In the *métro* car, Amanda's eyebrows rose at the number of vacant seats before she remembered it was only three in the afternoon — the earliest she'd left the office in four years. As the train stations passed before her eyes, a plan formed in her mind. She'd get home and locate her father's Swiss Army knife. Then she'd down a few shots of vodka, return to the office, kill Julien, and kill herself.

It sounded like an excellent plan.

Twenty minutes later, she pushed open the door to her apartment and went straight to the minibar, praying she hadn't imagined the bottle of vodka hiding behind her expensive wines.

Bingo!

There it was — cold to the touch and as real as the sharp pain in her heart.

She filled a glass with the transparent liquid and drained it. The beverage burned her tongue. Amanda yelled out a battle cry, jumped up and down a few times while punching the air, and poured herself another glass. She set it on the coffee table and retrieved a tub of chocolate ice cream from the freezer. With her glass in one hand and the ice cream in the other, she kicked off her shoes and settled into her creamy leather sofa — the one she'd bought on credit, like almost everything else in her stylish little apartment.

By the time she finished her second glass, Amanda's diabolical plan had begun to lose its appeal. Julien Barre deserved to die, for sure, but murder was a messy business.

And suicide—even more so.

She pictured herself on the floor, blood gushing from her punctured stomach and trickling from her mouth.

Ugh.

Besides, what if she failed to finish Julien off? Or herself? After all, the biggest creature she'd ever assassinated had been a cockroach. The act had been so disgusting it gave her nightmares for weeks.

Fine. No killing.

But then what? She couldn't just sit here and do nothing—she was a fighter. Amanda clenched her fists and willed her vodka-soaked gray matter to hatch up a plan B. As soon as her brain obliged, she stomped to the bedroom and dug her crimson femme fatale lipstick from her makeup case. She shoved her most elegant evening gown, a tee, and a pair of panties into an overnight bag and rushed out of her apartment.

Plan B was insane, but it was carnage-free.

A few meters down the street, Amanda withdrew as much cash as the ATM would give her, and hailed a cab.

"Where to, *madame*?" the driver asked as she slumped into the backseat.

"Gare Saint-Lazare, please." She pulled out her phone and added on an impulse, "I'm going to Deauville."

"A beach weekend?" He smiled into the mirror.

"Nope. A night of gambling at the casino," she said, flashing him her brightest smile.

The driver's eyebrows shot up before he returned his gaze to the road. He didn't offer a comment.

Amanda sat back and tapped "blackjack rules" into the search engine on her phone.

She had three hours to master the game.

* * *

By the time Amanda stepped into her hotel room, it was getting dark. She switched on the lights and surveyed her room.

Nice.

It had better be, considering the price she was paying for it. Royal Barrière was one of the town's best hotels, as grand and expensive as its name suggested. Was this reasonable? Certainly not. But tonight wasn't about reasonable. It was about winning big.

Besides, the thought of staying in a seedy hotel gave her goose bumps. She was no longer a discount-eligible, backpack-carrying student. She was twenty-eight — too old for seedy hotels. And, thankfully, not yet broke enough. Mind you, if everything went according to plan tonight, she wouldn't be broke at all.

The plan was simple, as all genius ideas were: exploit her beginner's luck.

Amanda was a gambling virgin, so new she still had her price tags. She'd never set foot in a casino or tried a slot machine. She'd never even played cards with friends.

Seeing as she had no friends.

She shook her head, brushing that thought away.

I do have friends. A whole bunch of them — because four counted as a bunch, right? And it was four more than she'd had ten years ago in her fat-padded, acne-decorated teens. Thank God, those days were gone. Now she was as slim, peach-skinned, and honey-blonde as the next self-respecting Parisian *it girl*. And, most importantly, she'd become the picture-perfect young lady her mother could parade in front of her friends.

As for Amanda's own friends, there was Karine, the PA from work who qualified thanks to the number of bitching sessions they'd shared over the years. Then there was Jeanne, a bartender, and Jeanne's fiancé, Mat, both of whom happened to be best friends with Amanda's ex. And finally, Patrick, business partner of said ex.

Amanda frowned at the annoying realization that three of her four friends were the legacy of her ex-boyfriend Rob.

Note to self: diversify my social circle.

She donned her strappy gown and refreshed her makeup. Then she grabbed her Chanel purse with her ID, cash, and the cocktail voucher the concierge had given her and headed to the famed Deauville Casino that adjoined her hotel.

Ten minutes into the game, Amanda began to suspect that her two-hour crash course on the train might have been insufficient. But it didn't matter because her beginner's luck should kick in any moment now.

She surveyed the players at her table to divert her mind from worrying.

What a motley crew!

Across from her sat an elderly Spanish couple. They wore matching T-shirts and smiled simultaneously, flashing their dentures. Next to them, two forty-something British women spoke to each other in an incomprehensible English dialect. A middle-aged Frenchman with greasy hair and darting eyes sat beside them. Amanda's neighbor to the left was a surgically enhanced bimbo of unknown provenance doused with a nauseating perfume and clad in a dress that was three sizes too small.

But the most remarkable person at the table was Amanda's neighbor to the right, whom she'd nicknamed Obsidian Eyes. In his late twenties, tall, swarthy, well built, and well dressed, the man was easy on the eyes. He wore a faux casual linen suit and played with the easy confidence of someone who knew what he was doing.

Amanda began to fidget with the strap of her watch, annoyed that the table blocked her view of his footwear. So many things could go wrong with the shoes! They could be synthetic or patent leather, have rubber soles, be coated in dirt or dust, sport pointy toes or toes that were too rounded . . . The list of potential offenses was long, and every one of them was unforgivable even with mitigating circumstances.

She was a bit of shoe fetishist.

Well, maybe a lot.

Overtaken by curiosity, Amanda discreetly pushed a card to the edge of the table until it fell to the floor. She bent down to pick it up and checked out the hunk's shoes so she could add him to her huge "discard" pile. But, to her surprise, Obsidian Eyes wore fine leather loafers that were flawless.

Probably Italian.

Handmade, without a doubt.

She sat up and studied his face again, perplexed. He had such fine eyes — intelligent and framed with extra thick lashes. The man was undeniably handsome, but not in a classic European way. Come to think of it, handsome wasn't the adjective she'd use to describe him. It didn't do him justice. It was too common, too weak. . . while he was kind of stunning.

His complexion and features held a touch of something exotic, faintly alien—something that kept her stealing glances at him whenever he turned his attention to his cards. Was it his wavy, jet-black hair, mesmerizing eyes, or chiseled jawline? Or maybe his exquisite eyebrows that made her think of a raven's wings? Whatever that *je ne sais quoi* was, it made him look more than ordinary. And hot.

The man was a blazing wildfire on legs.

As if his looks weren't enough, Obsidian Eyes played exceptionally well. Forty minutes into the game, his stacks of colorful chips had doubled while everyone else's—including Amanda's—had melted away.

That thought snapped her back into reality. Panicked, Amanda raised her eyes to the high ceiling of the casino.

Please, I can't lose.

She was gambling with her meager savings—half of it, to be exact. If the Supreme Being above intended to activate her beginner's luck, now was the time.

"Newbie?" Obsidian Eyes asked, his gaze never shifting from the deck in the dealer's hands.

He spoke French like a native. A slight Midi accent, maybe? A bit like Jeanne's, but less pronounced.

Amanda looked around, unsure whom he was talking to.

Obsidian Eyes finally lifted his gaze from the cards and gave her a panty-dropping smile.

She arched an eyebrow. "Does it show?"

"Mhmm."

Ooh, that smile again.

The dealer held up a card for her, and she started reaching for it when she noticed Obsidian Eyes give a quick shake of his head. She pulled back.

And won the hand.

"Thank you," she mouthed to her unexpected mentor.

He gave her a small nod.

She followed his discreet instructions for two more hands and won both. The evening was beginning to look up.

The dealer bowed and ceded his place to a good-looking young woman with sleek auburn hair smoothed back into the world's tightest bun.

She greeted the players and began to shuffle the cards.

Obsidian Eyes turned to Amanda. "Why blackjack? Beginners usually prefer the slots or roulette."

"I don't know . . . Too passive for me, I guess."

He nodded. "I avoid them, too."

"So you know what I mean."

"Yes. But that's not my only reason."

She cocked her head. "No?"

"The slots are twice as costly to players than the table games, and with roulette, too much depends on chance."

Amanda smirked. "Isn't that the case with all the games?"

"Not blackjack, if played right."

"Let me guess—*you* play it right."

He glanced at the dealer, who was engrossed in shuffling cards. "I know a trick or two."

One of the Brits stage-whispered to the other, "I hope he'll show me some of his tricks tonight." She paused before adding even louder, "In my room."

Both women burst out laughing.

Obsidian Eyes shifted uncomfortably and looked down at his hands, pretending he hadn't heard the saucy remark.

The man with greasy hair whispered something to the plastic bimbo.

She didn't acknowledge him. The woman was too busy multitasking. With her chest heaving, she stared at Obsidian Eyes and stroked her neck. Every five seconds she licked her lips and then pouted.

But the black-eyed hunk was oblivious to her onslaught. He turned to Amanda again. "I'm taking a break to stretch my legs."

"Er . . . OK."

He lowered his voice to a whisper. "I have a bad feeling about this dealer."

"Oh." She pushed her chips closer together like he had done and stood. "I'll do the same, then."

"What brings you to Deauville Casino tonight?" he asked as they strolled between the tables and observed the goings-on.

After a second's hesitation, she said, "I'm writing a book about gamblers."

"Participant observation, huh?"

Her eyebrows rose. "What do *you* know about participant observation?"

"Yeah, well, I need something to help me sleep when I get to my room at three in the morning." He shrugged. "Reading a few pages of *Tristes Tropiques* works better than any sleeping pill I've tried."

She giggled. "I'm passionate about cultural anthropology, but I could never finish that book."

"I like psychology books better," he said. "They're fun to read, and the info in them is useful in my trade."

"Oh?"

He nodded. "Especially books like Cialdini's *Influence* and the ones on how to read body language."

"I see."

"Hey, how about a glass of champagne on the terrace after I've won my target amount?" He gave her an innocent smile. A little too innocent.

"I have a cocktail voucher," she blurted before she could stop herself.

Did I just accept his invitation?

Oh, well. What harm could a drink do?

His face contorted in exaggerated disgust. "Trust me, you don't want their free cocktail unless you're a gustative masochist."

She put her hands on her hips. "I was given a free voucher, and I intend to use it."

"OK, OK. But don't say I didn't warn you."

She tilted her head to the side. "You said 'my target amount' earlier. Are you *that* good?"

"In all modesty . . . yes. But my target amount is also reasonable. And I have a spending threshold, too. When I reach it before I've won my target amount, I *always* stop."

"How very rational for a gambler!"

"I'm full of surprises, in case you haven't noticed." He gave her an appreciative look. "And I suspect that so are you, *ma belle*."

"When did I become your *belle*?"

"Oh, it's just a placeholder until you tell me your name."

Should I?

"So, what's your name, ma belle?"

"Am . . . elie. And yours?"

"Kes."

"What kind of name is Kes?"

"A Gypsy name."

"Like, a *real* Traveler Gypsy?"

"As authentic as they come."

"Ah." She raised her chin. "That explains it."

"Explains what, Amelie?"

"That you make me think of Tarzan."

"Really?"

"Not that you aren't dashing in your suit, but you look like someone who was born to ride horses bare-chested."

"Wow. You're the bluntest belle I've ever met."

"And you're the most gorgeous Gypsy I've ever met."

Where did that come from? Must be the vodka.

The corners of his mouth twitched. "So refreshingly honest. Why, I'm flattered."

She looked away.

Honest, my foot.

He wasn't just the most handsome Gypsy she'd ever seen—he was the most spectacular man, all ethnicities included.

Now, that *was honest.*

She turned to him and cleared her throat. "Shall we go back? Target amounts and all."

"Sure."

The sleek-haired dealer was leaving when they returned to their seats. Both giggling Brits and Greasy Hair were gone. The elderly couple and the bimbo still played, but judging by their dismal faces and the measly number of chips in front of them, they weren't doing well.

Kes had been right about the dealer.

"What does your gut tell you about this one?" Amanda eyed the middle-aged man who had taken over for his colleague.

"He's the best."

Her face fell.

Kes grinned. "Not for the house, ma belle, for us. Move closer so I can see your cards without twisting my neck."

She moved as close to him as their chairs allowed.

"Now relax and do exactly as I say."

Amanda glanced at Kes, but he had already turned his full attention to the cards.

* * *

For the next hour, they played in near silence. The few times Amanda tried to strike up a conversation, Kes shushed her with a smile and a whispered "counting for two here, remember?"

And count he did.

Amanda's job was easy: she hit when he said hit, stood when he said stand, and split her cards when he said split. Their chip stacks kept growing until Kes laid his palms on the table and mouthed to her, *Stop*.

She gave him a puzzled look. "Now?"

He nodded and then tipped the dealer. "I'm going to call it a night."

"But we're winning. Please, you can't stop now."

"Oh yes, I can." He leaned to whisper in her ear, "And so should you before they ask us to back off. Besides, this deck is becoming too hot."

She hesitated. The seven hundred euros she'd won wasn't the amount she'd been hoping for when she jumped on the train at Saint-Lazare. It would hardly solve her problems . . . but it would pay her mortgage next month. In spite of the alcohol in her system, Amanda knew she would've lost half her savings tonight had it not been for Kes. Continuing to play without him would be unwise.

"What about that drink you promised me?" he asked.

"Sure." She stood and smoothed her dress. "Lead the way, maestro."

He took her to the bar where they climbed onto tall barstools and ordered their drinks. The voucher cocktail was as bad as Kes had predicted it would be. Amanda winced at its candy taste and pushed the glass away.

"How about a mojito?" Kes asked. "It's one of their more decent concoctions."

She nodded.

As he passed her the glass, their fingertips brushed.

Amanda couldn't help noting how pleasant that contact was. Actually, *pleasant* was an understatement. It was electrifying.

Easy, girl. No one-night stands, remember?

"So, what is it like, the life of a gambler?" she asked.

"I'm not a gambler. Well, not in the usual sense, anyway."

"Oh, yes?"

"I'm a card counter. I've made a decent living from it for five years."

"How old are you?"

"Twenty-six."

"So you see this as a job?"

He nodded. "That's exactly how I see it. I have a job that I like and am good at."

She felt a sharp pang at his words.

Aren't you lucky?

"What's wrong, Amelie?"

"Nothing." She gave him one of her fake smiles. "And what about five years ago—what was your occupation then? Palm-reading or playing the accordion in the métro?"

He smirked. "So tactful and unprejudiced. Have you applied for sainthood yet?"

"You didn't answer my question."

"If you were trying to imply those are common Gypsy occupations, you're wrong. At least, as far as the French *Gitans* are concerned."

She arched an eyebrow.

"Gitan men are typically itinerant vendors or metalworkers," he said. "My dad, for example, deals in scrap metal. Some are lumbermen. The women are usually artisans or peddlers. In the fall, everyone is a grape picker. We don't engage in the trades you mentioned."

"Oh, I didn't realize Gitans were the Gypsy elite. Please forgive my ignorance."

He moved a little closer and flashed her a toothy smile. "I see you're determined to insult me. But here's the thing—I'm not easily insulted."

"Is that so?"

"We Gypsies are a thick-skinned lot." He shrugged. "Can't afford to be touchy."

She blushed, suddenly embarrassed. Had she been too rude? She had, but not out of prejudice. Well, not only out of prejudice. She was trying to drive him away so she wouldn't have to make tough decisions when they finished their drinks.

Still, he didn't deserve her spite—he *had* just saved her from aggravating her already precarious financial situation.

"I was impressed with your memory and your mental arithmetic," she said, offering him the olive branch of a sincere compliment.

"At school, I was good at math."

"Did you go to college?"

He shook his head. "I hadn't even considered it."

"Why not?"

"For one, a college education isn't something my family believes in. And then . . . I stumbled on this book at a flea market when I was seventeen."

"What book?"

"*The Blackjack System.* I read it in one day, reread it three more times, and then practiced with my cousin."

"Couldn't you practice online?"

"I did that, too. But the system works only with a finite number of decks on the table and a human dealer."

"I see."

"I couldn't wait to turn eighteen so I could go to a casino and put my skills to the test."

"And it worked?"

"Not immediately, but with time I got better. You see, the beauty of blackjack is that luck isn't the decisive factor. Luck determines the cards you're dealt. But it's your knowledge and skill that determine how you play them."

"Are you really making money on this?" She narrowed her eyes. "Like, regularly?"

"I've made a good profit in almost every casino I've played in. Except the ones that figure out too quickly I'm counting cards."

"So what happens once Deauville Casino figures you out?"

"They'll ban me, and I'll move on to play elsewhere."

"And when every casino in France has banned you?"

"I'll play in Belgium, Switzerland, Italy, Germany, Spain, Portugal . . . Or I'll go to Vegas and then to Asia. The world is big."

"So that's your life plan?"

"You could say that."

She drained her mojito.

He beckoned to the bartender and then turned to Amanda. "Any food allergies or diet restrictions?"

"No. Why?"

"We'll have two cold cuts and cheese plates, please," he said to the barman.

When they swallowed the last slices of spicy chorizo, Kes asked matter-of-factly, "My hotel or yours?"

Oh Lord. There it was—decision time. But wait a minute. Why was she even considering it? She didn't do one-night stands. She wasn't that kind of girl. What she needed to do was wish him good night in her poshest accent and leave.

It was the only reasonable move.

Except . . . she wasn't being reasonable tonight. Right now, she was curious and thrilled. Her heart fluttered with anticipation. She all but drooled over the juicy exotic fruit that was this man. Just this once she itched to be wanton. After all, her reputation in that department was so unnaturally pristine it was begging for a stain.

And just like that, Amanda made up her mind: she was going to bed with Kes, the gambler she'd met a few hours ago.

He bit into his last pickle. "Do you have a boyfriend?"

"No. Do you?"

"Believe it or not, I've never had a boyfriend." His eyes crinkled with amusement. "I'm a virgin that way."

She chuckled.

He broke into an infectious grin before adding in a more serious tone, "No girlfriend at the moment, either."

"Do you have a condom?" she heard herself ask.

He blinked and then nodded. "Yep—in my room. My hotel then?"

"Only if it's decent."

"As decent as it gets in this town. I'm staying at Royal Barrière—it's the building next door."

Was his being at the same hotel as she was a sign, a green light of sorts? She could sneak out and go to her room as soon as the deed was done—a perfect setup for a hassle-free, controlled bit of fun. If she were ever going to have her first one-night stand, there wouldn't be a better occasion.

He must have seen the outcome of her expeditious debate on her face because he took her hand and led her from the bar.

End of Excerpt

About the Author

Alix Nichols is an unapologetic caffeine addict and a longtime fan of Mr. Darcy, especially in his Colin Firth incarnation. She is an award-winning author of sexy romantic comedies.

At the age of six, she released her first rom com. It featured highly creative spelling on a dozen pages stitched together and bound in velvet paper.

Decades later, she still loves the romance genre. Her spelling has improved (somewhat), and her books have made bestseller lists in the US, UK and France, climbing as high as #1. She lives in France with her family and their almost-human dog.

Connect with her online:

Blog: **http://www.alixnichols.com**
Facebook: **www.facebook.com/AuthorAlixNichols**
Twitter: **twitter.com/aalix_nichols**
Pinterest: **http://www.pinterest.com/AuthorANichol s**
Goodreads: **goodreads.com/alixnichols**

Made in the USA
Middletown, DE
30 April 2017